PRAISE FOR *CAN*

"*Can You Hear Us Now?* is an inspiring tale of midlife women living, and loving, and making act three their best season of all."

~Joan Lunden, journalist, *New York Times* bestselling author, health & wellness advocate

"As the creator of the Three Tomatoes, Cheryl Benton has her finger on the cultural pulse of the midlife and beyond woman. In her latest novel, she highlights and celebrates mature women. And more importantly, she reveals this stage of life with entertaining, nuanced and complex female characters, showing us the modern woman's story doesn't end in her thirties. In Cheryl's literal world, women of all ages, are fully living their best lives."

~Dr. Robi Ludwig, nationally known psychotherapist and award-winning reporter, author of *Your Best Age is Now*

"Encouraging and perfectly titled, *Can You Hear Us Now*? is an anthem for all 'women of a certain age' that declares opportunity and fun await us in our fifties and beyond. Cheryl Benton brilliantly draws us into the exciting lives of three glamorous best friends, their husbands, lovers, professional ambitions, and relatable challenges as they help each other overcome adversity. I enjoyed this page-turner —as will you!

~ Dian Griesel, founder, Silver Disobedience® Inc., Wilhelmina model, author of *The Silver Disobedience Playbook.*

"*Can You Hear Us Now*? is a fabulously fun, energetic, sexy and stylish follow-up to *Can You See Us Now*?. It takes us through all the major touchpoints of life after fifty: change, loss, ageism, opportunity, career, relationships, sex, and especially, friendship. These chic women are fearless, confident, and uber-cool but when they have occasional moments of doubt, they know exactly what to do: get together for a martini (or two), laugh, cry, and most of all, talk it through."

~Barbara Hannah Grufferman, author, *Love Your Age: The Small-Step Solution to a Better, Longer, Happier Life,* and a leading voice for positive aging.

"Love love loved this relatable, inspirational and wildly entertaining tale of women just like us navigating the shoals of life and taking no prisoners! Put your life on hold to read this delicious, page-turning slice of life—and come out infinitely enriched! A joyful romp. The movie version cannot be far behind!"

~Judy Katz, author, ghostwriter, critic

CAN YOU HEAR US NOW?

A Novel

Cheryl Benton

Author of *Can You See Us Now?*

Published July 2021

ISBN: 978-1-7364949-7-4
Library of Congress Control Number: 2021913387

For information address:
The Three Tomatoes Book Publishing
6 Soundview Rd.
Glen Cove, NY 11542

Web address: www.thethreetomatoespublishing.com

Cover photo: iStock
Cover graphics and interior design: Susan Herbst
Author's photo: Annie Watt

DEDICATION

To my family and friends, you are even more cherished after
the challenging times we have all experienced.
And to my dear friend Bruce Matthews, and the millions of
people who did not make it through the pandemic,
you hold a special place in my heart.
These staggering losses remind us that growing older is a gift
and every moment should be celebrated.

"And if tomorrow never comes, I will die happily knowing that I was one of the fortunate ones who found true love, that I was one of the lucky ones who had friends beside me in the good times and the bad times. And I will die happily knowing that I was far from perfect, but I gave it my best. Please do not weep for me when I am gone, but remember me with smiles and laughter when you think about the good times we have shared and toast me with a perfectly dry martini from time to time as well."

CHAPTER 1
RETURN TO THE LIVING

Suzy looked at herself in the mirror. Really looked at herself, for the first time since Ken's death six months earlier. Her cheeks had a hollowness she hadn't noticed before. The dark circles under her eyes bore the telltale signs of many sleepless nights. And her hair. My God, what had happened to her hair? It looked as lifeless as she felt. "Well, this won't do," Suzy said out loud, and then realized she was talking only to herself. And then the reality set in. If she was going to meet up tonight with her two best friends, Madge and Trish, for martinis and then join their group of friends for dinner, she was going to have to whip herself into shape.

She slowly made her way down the stairs from the penthouse to the next level of the loft that housed the offices of The Three Tomatoes, the media company she had founded with Madge and Trish to celebrate women over forty-five. She found Amy, their CEO, at one of the small conference tables.

"Amy, I'm in desperate need of a makeover before I meet Madge and Trish tonight, but I just can't bring myself to go to my usual salon and face condolences again. Any ideas of where I might get into today?"

Amy looked at her boss and was so relieved to see the old Suzy starting to come back. "I've got just the place. It's the hottest new salon in the city and it's right here in Tribeca. Let me see what I can do."

Thirty minutes later Suzy was being greeted by Alphonso, the latest hairstylist darling of celebrities and models. "Ciao, bella, what can we do for you today?" he asked as he air-kissed both her cheeks.

"I'm in your hands. Whatever you think." Suzy actually shocked herself with that statement, since she rarely ventured out of her comfort zone of the long straight blond highlighted hairstyle she had worn for years—just the way Ken had loved it.

~~~~~~~

Madge and Trish were seated at a cocktail table near the fireplace in Campbell Apartment, an elegant cocktail lounge with a great history, hidden away in Grand Central Terminal. Their martinis had just arrived.

"I'm glad we decided to meet a little earlier before Suzy arrives," said Madge. "I know seeing the group tonight might be a little overwhelming, so let's keep a close eye on her."

"I did reach out to everyone and they've promised to keep the evening light and upbeat," said Trish. "But I think it's a good sign that she actually agreed to come tonight."

Trish and Madge were still in shock themselves over Ken's sudden death. He and Suzy had been married for nearly thirty years and had been one of those truly charmed couples. Lovers and best friends, who also looked beautiful as a couple—
~~~~~~~

they'd been dubbed "Ken and Barbie." Trish and Madge had been bridesmaids at their wedding. Neither of them would ever forget the call that day from Ian, Ken and Suzy's son, telling them that Ken had collapsed from an aneurism on the tennis court and died instantly. Beautiful, kind, smart, perfect Ken. Even now it was hard to believe.

They had rushed to be at her side. Suzy was in disbelief and went through the motions of comforting her two children, Ian and Keri, while stoically greeting the hundreds of mourners who poured into the church and then back to Suzy and Ken's home after the funeral. Everyone commented on how well she was holding up. Three days later Ian and Keri, at their mother's urging, left to return to their lives. That was when Suzy fell apart.

Trish and Madge rushed to her side and packed a few of her things and took their best friend to Madge and her husband, Jason's, farm in Vermont. Suzy stayed there for the next month under the watchful eye of their housekeeper, Bertha. Trish and Madge would have stayed the whole time, but Suzy insisted they get back to their lives too, so they limited themselves to weekend visits.

It was on the fourth weekend that Suzy decided she had to get back and that work was what she needed. Since the founding of The Three Tomatoes, the company had grown to the point that they now had a CEO and a full-time staff, and the three of them were the board members. Suzy, who liked being hands-on remained as chair, and Madge and Trish were able to contribute to the parts of the business they were most passionate about. For Madge, it was the documentary film group she had created under the company's media umbrella, and for Trish it was art and being an advocate for healthy living. Madge, now raising a family with Jason, appreciated the flexibility. And Trish was thinking about exploring the art world again, which had always been her first passion. So, Suzy had become the day-to-day person overseeing the company, which worked well for all.

"Are you sure you're ready?" Trish and Madge had queried her.

"I don't know that I'll ever be ready, but I think it's a start. But I do have a request."

"Anything," they both said in unison.

"I'm not ready to go back to the house in Bronxville, in fact I'm not sure if I ever will be. So, do you think I can stay in the loft apartment, until I figure out my next steps?"

The apartment was on the top floor of a beautifully restored Romanesque revival building that had been the offices of Jason Madison, Madge's husband, for his start-up tech company that eventually made him a billionaire. He had converted the top floor into an apartment that he stayed in when he wasn't at his farm in Vermont. After he sold his company, he gave his offices to The Three Tomatoes. When he and Madge got married and adopted two children from Ethiopia, they bought a brownstone in Brooklyn, so the apartment was rarely used.

And so it was that Suzy went back to work, and the office and the loft apartment became her refuge. She had barely left the premises, only when Madge and Trish insisted that they at least stroll to a quiet neighborhood restaurant for a meal. So, tonight was a big deal and they were both concerned.

"You started without me?" laughed Suzy as she arrived at their table.

Trish and Madge, who had been deep in conversation, looked up startled and then both gasped.

"Oh my God, look at you, Suzy—I barely recognize you," said Trish. And neither did Madge.

Suzy's long blond hair had been cut into a chic bob with bangs and was a shade lighter. Her beautiful blue eyes sparkled in a way they hadn't in months, and she was wearing a sexy black leather sheath and her trademark Louboutins.

"Well, I hope you mean that in a good way, and where the hell is my martini?"

They all laughed and then teared up a bit. For a moment it felt like old times.

CHAPTER 2
BACK IN THE FOLD

The Ripe Tomatoes were back at their usual iconic Broadway restaurant for their monthly dinners that had become a ritual for several years now. The group was originally started by their friend Hope (a Tony-winning Broadway producer) to bring together some of the amazing women she knew in New York City. While age was never the criteria, accomplishments and substance were, which usually required a few years of living to obtain.

It was around their third dinner together when their usual waiter looked at them appreciatively and said, "This is a group of hot tomatoes." When he left, Trish had been the first to ask, "What's a tomato?" It was Celeste, the oldest in the group, who explained that in her day, that's what guys called a savvy, sexy woman of a 'certain age' who knows her way around a man and a martini too. They all laughed when Hope chuckled and said they were certainly a group of ripe tomatoes, and the name stuck.

When Suzy, Madge, and Trish were invited into the group five years earlier, they had just turned fifty and were starting to feel like their options in life were running out. Each went through a turning point crisis that ultimately led them to start The Three Tomatoes, and let other women know they were not alone in feeling invisible and marginalized because they were past fifty. Their mission was to change the perception of aging and celebrate growing older. And the Ripe Tomatoes had been there to inspire them and cheer them on, every step of the way.

Surrounded by their friendship and love, Suzy was glad she had joined them tonight. They had all gone out of their way to keep the evening fun and light.

"Darling, that haircut and color are absolutely divine," said Hope at the start of the evening, and the entire group concurred. "How did you ever get an appointment with Alphonso himself? He's usually booked for months."

"If I tell you, I'd have to kill you," Suzy laughed. "But thank you all for the compliments. I'm still not sure it's me, but then again, I'm not sure who me is now." She paused. "Oh God, that was maudlin. I need another martini and I need to know what you're all up to these days."

"Well, I'm still looking for the next *If Tomorrow Never Comes* so Broadway doesn't think I'm a one-Tony wonder," said Hope. "Celeste, ever since you married that handsome Brit with a title and went off to live happily-ever-after we don't have your dating escapades as creative sparks."

Celeste laughed. She was nearing eighty now and was still churning out a best-selling romance novel every year. It was one of her dating adventures with a ninety-six-year-old billionaire that ultimately turned into the Tony-award-winning show and won Celeste a Tony award as playwright. And that same year, she married anther best-selling novelist, Sir Oliver

Spence and divided her time between his manor home outside London and her New York City apartment.

"I may be boring these days, but let me tell you this. Now that I'm spending so much time in England in Oliver's circle of friends, several of whom are close to the royals, there are so many scandalous rumors, it makes New York City sound provincial."

"Well, spill the beans, Lady Spence," said Madge.

And with that, Celeste lowered her voice and shared a story about a royal threesome that had them all enthralled. "But you are not to breathe a word of this," she said when she finished her tale, which may have been just that.

The wine flowed, and the conversation was fun, and by the end of the evening Suzy felt like she had been embraced in the warmest hug that stayed with her even as she returned to the loft apartment. She poured herself a small glass of brandy, Ken's favorite after dinner drink, and strolled out onto the terrace. She looked out at the city on this sparkling autumn evening and lifted her glass to the sky with a silent toast to Ken. That was when she noticed the cardinal perched on the terrace railing. *Where did that come from?* she thought. But that's when she knew exactly what she had to do next.

~~~~~~

Madge quietly walked into the entryway of the Brooklyn brownstone she shared with her husband, Jason, (twelve years her junior) and their two beautiful children. Madge still had to pinch herself with this wondrous twist her life had taken. To think that just a few short years ago she was single, with no thoughts of ever marrying again, and miserable in her
~~~~~~

TV morning anchor job.

Just as she was hanging up her coat, Jason appeared with Maggie, their golden Lab, following on his heels. *God, it never gets old,* she thought as her heart beat a little faster as this gorgeous man embraced her in a bear hug. And to think how she had pushed him away in the beginning because of the age difference, which only she saw as a problem.

"The kids are fast asleep. Get comfy and join me in the den. I'll pour us a nightcap. I want to hear about the evening."

Madge went upstairs and changed quickly into a pair of silk pajamas and then peeked into the children's rooms. Her heart was bursting with love for these two precious ones she and Jason had adopted from an orphanage in Ethiopia. She kissed each gently on the head, first Yonas who was nine now and then she headed to six-year-old Bitania's room. *They're growing up so fast*, she thought as she went back downstairs.

Jason had a fire going on this cool fall evening and poured each of them a port. "So, tell me, how was Suzy?"

"I think she's finally coming back to the land of the living. She even got a fabulous new haircut, and she seemed to really enjoy the evening. She's agreed to come to the farm for Thanksgiving and Ian will come along too. And he has Elsa for the weekend, which will give Bitania a chance to play big sister. Suzy is disappointed though that Keri's decided to stay in Boston with her boyfriend, but I know how much Keri idolized her dad, so I think it's just too painful for her this year."

"It will be nice to have a full house with them, along with Trish and Michael and of course my mom and dad," Jason said as he pulled Madge in closer to him. "Do you know how much I love you, Mrs. Madison?" He leaned in and gave her a long passionate kiss.

"Let's take this upstairs, Mr. Madison."

~~~~~~

Across the river and uptown in Harlem, Trish was having a similar conversation with Michael.

"It's good to hear that Suzy's engaging with the world again," said Michael. "It's still so hard to believe he's gone. We spent so many wonderful Thanksgivings together. But it will be good for all of us to go to the farm this year."

"Yes. I know Suzy is dreading the holidays, but the farm is truly a healing oasis. Oh, and on another subject, I heard from one of Tania's sisters in Montego Bay. It seems her niece is a very talented artist like her aunt Tania, and she's starting graduate school at Parsons. She asked if I would meet her and keep a watchful eye on her. So, I thought I'd invite her to dinner this weekend, if that's okay with you?"

"Of course. Although I'm not sure how many graduate school students want a watchful eye on them, but from what I've observed being on the Columbia campus for a few years now, some of them could use that," Michael laughed. He was chair of a graduate program at Columbia University and had a lot more experience with this generation than she did.

"Well, it will be lovely to meet Tania's niece and see if she did indeed inherit some of that talent. And I'm sure she'll appreciate a home-cooked meal. I'll email her right now."

Trish had realized lately that she was really missing the art world. For years she had owned a gallery in the West Village where she had discovered several wonderful emerging artists. Tania had been her most successful discovery, a beautiful Black woman originally from Jamaica, who hadn't started
~~~~~~

painting until she was in her midsixties. Trish was instantly taken with Tania's energy and her incredible watercolors when she saw them on display at a sidewalk art fair. Tania had just turned eighty when Trish created her first gallery exhibition. Her work sold out in a week.

When she died six years later, the latest watercolors she had been working on sold for over one million dollars in a one-night gallery memorial tribute. The money went to fund art programs in Jamaica. That was the day Trish walked away from the gallery, once a source of joy, but now mostly full of painful memories. But as much as she loved The Three Tomatoes and the health and wellness programs she had created, along with the women's integrated health center she had helped spearhead, thanks to Jason and Madge's foundation grant, she felt the siren call of the art world.

CHAPTER 3
GOODBYES AND HELLOS

The day after the Ripe Tomatoes dinner, Suzy had texted Ian and Keri and asked if they would meet her at the Bronxville house the following weekend. They had barely been back to the house since the funeral. Suzy had returned a few times to check on the house and pick up clothes. Ian, who was now living in the East Village and attending law school at NYU, had gone with her on some of those occasions. Keri had returned to Boston after the funeral and hadn't been home since. Now, here they were sitting in the den. Ian had made a fire, but Suzy still felt chilled to the bone.

"I've made a decision, but I wanted to tell you both about it in person. I'm going to sell the house."

"You're what?" Keri stood up and yelled. "You can't do that. This is the house we grew up in. It's the house with all our memories of Dad."

Suzy was somewhat stunned by Keri's reaction, and they all sat there in silence for a few moments.

"Keri, listen," Ian broke the silence. "This is Mom's decision to make. You haven't lived in this house since you left home for college, and that was eight years ago."

"Yes, but it's still our house," Keri lashed back.

Suzy found her voice. "Keri, you're right. It's a house full of beautiful memories—of you and Ian growing up in this house. Of all the wonderful times with your father in this house. Those memories are ones we'll hold inside of us forever. But I can't live in a house that feels lifeless now, and I can't keep this house as a mausoleum to your father. He'd be the last one to want that."

"Mom's right, Keri. We're both off living our own lives now, and she needs to do that too."

Keri sat there with tears running down her cheeks. Suzy went over, sat beside her, and held her close, just like she would do when Keri was a child with a scraped knee.

They ordered pizza that night, and ate it in the den by the fire. They shared some of their favorite stories of Ken and laughed and cried. Suzy told them they could take whatever they wanted from the house and she would even hold some things in storage for them until they had houses of their own. The next day she hugged her children, and they said their goodbyes to the house. As soon as they left, she called a Realtor friend and put the house on the market.

~~~~~~

It was the first Tuesday of the month and Suzy, Trish, and Madge were assembled at the large conference table on the third floor of the loft for their monthly board meeting. Amy had updated them on the essentials—their latest subscriber growth, sponsorships, their current P&L, and their revenue
~~~~~~

projections. While subscribers and revenue were down a bit compared to the previous year, they were not particularly concerned. As Amy explained, they were getting to that point where their subscriber base starts to max out and then there's always attrition. They had grown quickly in a short period of time and this was a normal leveling out.

After Amy left, Suzy said, "There's one other thing you should know about. I got an inquiry last week that a very large streaming media company that's been in serious acquisition mode would like to have a conversation with us. Before I tell them we are not for sale, I thought we should discuss it first."

"Well, of course we're not for sale," said Trish. But then they both looked at Madge, who seemed to be mulling the idea. "Well, we're not for sale, are we?" asked Trish.

"Actually," said Madge with a pause. "I don't think we should say never, and while we may not be ready to sell, it doesn't hurt to listen to what a potential suitor has to say."

"Why would a big streaming media company even be interested in us?" queried Trish.

"Because we have a large subscriber base of a highly sought out demographic—women over fifty with disposable incomes and Madge's award-winning documentaries," said Suzy. "And the streaming media companies are all about getting the greatest number of paying subscribers so they can become king of the new entertainment mountain."

"Hmm...I hadn't thought of it that way. Maybe we should find some time over Thanksgiving weekend to talk about this. And we do have two great advisors to bring into the conversation—Michael with his Wall Street background, and Jason who built a start-up company and sold it."

"Agree," said Suzy.

"Me too," said Madge.

"How about we head up to the apartment and have a glass of wine and catch up?" Suzy suggested.

"So, what's happening with the sale of the house, and have you thought about where you want to live?" asked Madge once they were settled in with their vino.

"The Realtor is confident I'll get my asking price, but of course nothing will happen 'til after the holidays. I have looked at a fabulous apartment in one those new luxury high-rises in Midtown. It's like hotel living—everything is there at the push of a button. After years of living in and maintaining a house, I really like that idea. And it has three bedrooms, which is perfect for when Keri and Ian and little Elsa come and visit me. If the Realtor is right, and I get my price for the house, I think I can swing it."

Trish and Madge were happy to see Suzy visualizing a new future for herself.

"Trish, tell us all about Tania's niece," said Madge.

"Oh, she is wonderful. Her name is Tatiana—a nod to her aunt—and she is beautiful and has so much potential as an artist. Tania would be so proud of her. We've had her over twice for dinner, and I visited her on campus to see her art. And Madge, I wanted to ask you if you have room for one more at the farm? She's never had an American Thanksgiving."

"Of course," said Madge. "The more the merrier. And I can't wait to meet her."

CHAPTER 4

THANKSGIVING AT THE FARM

By Wednesday evening everyone had arrived safely at the farm and in time for the pizza that Jason had ordered from a new pizza parlor, which he had pronounced as not New York City pizza, but pretty darn good. Ian had volunteered to go with him in the pickup truck. Jason was glad to get a chance to catch up with him and see how he was doing since his dad's death.

"So, how's law school going?" asked Jason.

"I'm glad to be in the home stretch. I already have an offer to join Dad's old law firm, but I'm not sure corporate law is my thing. I don't think I want a pity job offer either."

"I hear you're at the top of your class, Ian, so I doubt it's a pity offer, and I'm sure there will be lots more offers. I can understand how you might not want to go into corporate law, but there are lots of other types of law you could practice."

"The thing is, I'm not really sure I want to be a lawyer. Dad was so excited when I first mentioned going to law school. He had this dream of my joining the firm, and I didn't want to let him down. But to be honest, I'm now realizing it was his dream, and not really mine."

Ian never ceased to amaze Jason with his maturity and insights. It couldn't have been easy for him to become a father at eighteen. He was determined to not only support his daughter, but to stay in her life, which he has done, even though the romantic relationship with her mother ended. He also finished Princeton in four years and was completing law school.

"Just know I'm here anytime if you want to talk."

"Thanks, Jason. I really appreciate it. So, what's the story with Tatiana?"

"Ah, so I see you noticed her," laughed Jason. Which was an understatement. Ian had barely taken his eyes off her since she arrived at the farm. "Well, I think that will be a great conversation to have over pizza."

~~~~~~

The pizza dinner had been crazy, chaotic fun. The kids were all wound up, and Bitania and Elsa had dressed as Disney princesses for dinner. The girls had immediately gravitated to Tatiana, who entertained them by drawing sketches of each of them.

"I think it's time that three certain children make their way to bed," said Madge.

"I would love to volunteer for that job," said Elizabeth, Jason's mom.

"Ian, let me get Elsa to bed," Suzy chimed in. "I love spending time with her."

And with that, the two loving grandmas made their way upstairs with two little princesses and a reluctant Yonas who
~~~~~~

wanted to stay up later.

"Who's up for a game or two of pool?" asked Jason.

A few minutes later, Jason escorted his dad, John, Michael, Trish, Madge, and Tatiana to the apartment over the garage—once his sister, Chrissy's, apartment—and now a pool hall since she married and moved out.

Jason poured drinks for everyone and cued up the rack.

"All right, Dad, I'm challenging you," said Madge.

Everyone was having a great time watching each player step up to the table to be the next champion. Tatiana had quietly watched from the sidelines, until Ian was last man standing, and she was the only one left to challenge him.

She walked up to the table quietly and chalked her stick. Ian set up the rack and said, "Okay, Tatiana, the goal is to make sure you don't get the eight ball into a pocket."

And with that condescending remark, Tatiana picked up her stick, unracked the balls, and proceeded to run the table.

The group laughed and applauded at the same time.

"Well, Ian, I think you have some crow to eat," said Jason. "And Tatiana, how the heck did you become a pool shark?"

"Simple. I was the only girl with four brothers, and I always had to compete."

"Okay, Tatiana, we're going to have to have a rematch to save my dignity. Best out of three," said Ian.

"Well, I'm packing it in. We have big day tomorrow," said Madge. And the rest of the group soon said their good-nights too.

"All right, show me what you got," said Ian, when they were finally alone. Tatiana beat him two out of three.

"This calls for a beer," he said handing Tatiana a cold bottle from a local Vermont brewery, and they clinked bottles.

"Your daughter is so precious. Trish told me some of your story, and I really admire that you are so involved in your daughter's life."

Ian sat down next to Tatiana, and for the next two hours they shared their life stories with each other.

He told her how his high school girlfriend, Emily, got pregnant when they both came home for Thanksgiving break their freshman year in college. They realized it was a mistake and broke up before heading back to their respective colleges. And then three months later Emily realized she was pregnant. They both knew they wanted to keep the baby and agreed, with the help of both sets of parents, to finish college.

"And we really, really tried to make it work," said Ian, "but by the time we graduated college we had both changed and wanted different things. But we've stayed friends and we co-parent Elsa."

Tatiana then told Ian about growing up in Jamaica with four older brothers. "We didn't have a lot of money, but we had a lot of love. And I always loved art, and my aunt Tania always encouraged me, and often brought me to visit her in New York City. She wanted me to do my undergraduate work in New York, but then I got a scholarship to the Royal College of Art in London, which was a wonderful opportunity. But I always knew I wanted to return to New York and when Parsons offered me a scholarship for their graduate program, my dream came true."

They continued talking effortlessly—what music they liked, their favorite hangouts in the city—when Tatiana said reluctantly, "Well, it's late, and I really must say good night."

"Okay, we'll head back to the house," said Ian as they slowly made their way down the steps of the garage. When they got outside, Ian stopped, and just looked at Tatiana in the moonlight. She was the most beautiful girl he had ever seen. And when she gazed back at him, he stepped forward, and placed his hands on the side of her cheeks and gave her the gentlest of kisses.

~~~~~~

They all did their best on Thanksgiving to keep the day upbeat, even though they had heavy hearts to be celebrating without Ken. For so many years, Madge, Trish, and Michael had gathered at Ken and Suzy's. It had always been one of Ken's favorite days and he did all the cooking. They got through the day, and they got Suzy and Ian through the day, but they were all glad when Friday came.

John and Elizabeth had planned a day for all the grandchildren. Chrissy had offered to take Ian and Tatiana on a long horseback riding adventure. So, the timing was perfect for Suzy, Trish, and Madge to talk about the potential suitor for The Three Tomatoes with Michael and Jason.

Michael weighed in with excellent advice on what to look for in a good deal and some of the things that were important to negotiate going in.

And Jason brought an interesting perspective as well.

"Listen, Snazzed was my baby," he said about the start-up that ultimately made him his billions. "But I had done what I wanted to do with it, and once it realized its potential, I had lost interest. I was more than ready to sell and walk away and let someone else take it in a new direction. My question to you three is, are you ready to do that? Are you ready to give up control?"
~~~~~~

They looked at each other and admitted they weren't really sure yet. But they also agreed they would proceed with a listening session from their suitors.

~~~~~~

By noon on Sunday, they were all packed and heading back home. Elizabeth and John were going home to Boston. Ian and Tatiana gave each other a bit too long of a hug, that no one failed to notice before Tatiana headed back to New York City with Trish and Michael.

As Ian was gathering up Elsa's things, Suzy flung her arms around Madge and Jason. "I don't have the words to say how much being here this weekend meant to Ian and me," and they all teared up and hugged each other tight.

Suzy realized she had just gotten through the first of many firsts without Ken.

On the drive back to New York City, Suzy started thinking about the next firsts without Ken—Christmas and New Year's. And then she had a brainstorm.

"Ian, I know Elsa will be with her mom over Christmas, so what if you and Keri and I, and Chris too if he likes, spend the holidays in Aspen?"

"Great idea, Mom. We haven't skied together in a long time. But how will we get a place in Aspen on this short notice?"

"I think I might have just the place."

When Suzy returned to the loft that night, she sent an email to Margot Tuttinger inviting her to dinner that week. Margot had just returned from London, but responded immediately. "My dear Suzy, I will be there with bells on."
~~~~~~

CHAPTER 5
THE CORPORATE SUITS

Margot Tuttinger had become a dear friend and mentor to Suzy. Margot was a legend in the beauty industry and had trusted Suzy and The Three Tomatoes to relaunch the beloved Arpello Perfume. They turned it into a retro revival success that won advertising acclaim and gave credibility to The Three Tomatoes as a marketing vehicle. Two years ago, Margot made the decision to retire as president of one of the largest beauty brands in the world.

They settled into a quiet corner in a little French bistro near Margot's Upper East Side brownstone.

"Oh, Suzy, it is so good to see you looking well. And your hairstyle is stunning."

"Well, coming from you, Margot, that's a supreme compliment. How are you finding life away from the big corporate madness?"

"You know over the years, I could never picture the day when I wasn't in the thick of it. Then one day I actually looked out the window at the fabulous view from my office on the fifty-third floor and realized there was a beautiful world out there that I wasn't living in, and it just felt like the right time. Of course, I'm still involved in a couple of corporate boards I sit on, and my philanthropic work, but the freedom of getting to choose what I want to do each day is a glorious feeling I never anticipated. I'm luxuriating in it. Now tell me about you, and of course, The Three Tomatoes."

"Oh, Margot, it's so very, very difficult. I'm trying to keep up the facade of being okay, but it gets exhausting. Everyone says it will get easier with time, but right now that feels like a platitude."

Margot took Suzy's hands into hers. "Grief doesn't have a timetable, and everyone grieves differently—just be kind to yourself and allow your emotions to be what they are. Is there anything I can do to help you?"

Suzy brushed a tear away. "Thank you for always saying the right thing. Actually, I do have a favor."

"Anything!"

"I know you don't usually use your Aspen home during Christmas week, and I was wondering if the kids and I could spend the holidays there this year?"

"Of course, you can. I think that is a wonderful idea, and a change of scenery is just what you all need. I'll make sure the house is ready for you. Now, tell me about The Three Tomatoes, and of course Trish and Madge."

Suzy caught her up, including telling her about the potential suitor.

"I think Madge is right. There's no harm in listening and just like with a man, it's always nice to feel pursued, although it's been a long time since I've been pursued. And I'm always happy to be a sounding board."

"They're pushing for a meeting before the holidays, so we'll see."

~~~~~~

It was the week after Thanksgiving, and Suzy, Madge, and Trish were being escorted into a sunlit conference room on one of the top floors of the Freedom Tower. This was headquarters of North Star Entertainment, one of the fastest growing streaming media companies.

"Mr. Greene and Mr. Katz will be with you in just a moment. Please help yourselves to coffee and tea, and water of course," said the lovely young assistant, "and let me know if you need anything else."

"Not too shabby," said Madge as they all gazed out of the floor-to-ceiling windows and the incredible views of Manhattan from south to north.

"We can't resist the view either," boomed a voice in back of them. The trio turned around.

"I'm Matt...and this is my partner, Stan. We are so excited to meet the Tomatoes! Please, have a seat."

Two hours later, the trio was seated at one of the little bistros inside Le District, the French marketplace in Battery Park. The waiter had just brought them a bottle of *rosé* and poured the first glasses.

Trish was the first to speak. "I have to say, I am feeling a little overwhelmed and I'm still reeling from their offer."

Madge and Suzy nodded in agreement.

"We're going to need time to digest this, but it sounds almost too good to be true, and you know what they say about that," said Suzy after a long sip of her wine. "But the resources
~~~~~~

they're offering up could catapult us into the stratosphere."

"The opportunity to have a ready-made distribution outlet of their scope for our documentaries is really mind-blowing," added Madge.

"I also like how important they feel our vision and staying true to it is for this venture to be successful," said Trish. "And the fact that we can still have ongoing roles in The Three Tomatoes and a voice in its future was a huge selling point for me."

Their salads arrived and they ate in silence for a few minutes.

"Madge," Suzy said, "I'm glad you encouraged us to meet with them. I liked what I heard too, but I just wish they weren't pushing us into making a decision so soon."

"You're right, Suzy. But we don't have to give them an answer until after the New Year. That will give us all time to think this through more, and have our lawyers look at the offer and the contracts. And of course, have Michael and Jason review everything too. But it is exciting!"

Trish raised her glass. "Well, let's toast to new opportunities in the New Year, whatever they may be!" And they all clinked glasses.

~~~~~~

The three weeks leading up to Christmas were a blur for Suzy. She had a generous offer on the Bronxville house and made the decision to buy the condo in the luxury Midtown high-rise. All of which would happen shortly after the first of the year. There had been endless conversations with Madge and Trish, with Michael and Jason weighing in when asked, and meet-
~~~~~~

ings with their lawyers to review the offer in greater detail.

But today, just two days before Christmas, they had agreed that just the three of them would meet at the apartment at the loft in the late afternoon to discuss all the pros and cons. They didn't want the decision weighing on them over the holidays. They arranged for dinner to be delivered from one of their favorite Italian restaurants in the neighborhood so they could celebrate whatever the outcome and the upcoming holidays.

Suzy had her easels out with large note pads for their discussion when Trish and Madge arrived.

"So, we've agreed that the only way we'll proceed with this offer is if we all three feel it's in the best interest of The Three Tomatoes, and in the best interest of each of us personally. And if any one of us doesn't feel it's the right thing to do, we nix the deal."

"Absolutely," said Trish. "It's all or none."

"Madge, let's start with your list of the pros." Suzy started filling in the easel pad.

Two hours later, they had filled two easel pads of pros and cons. And while the pros outweighed the cons, they spent most of the time discussing the cons and really listening to each other's concerns.

When they felt they had finally exhausted their lists, Suzy said, "Okay, ladies, it is time to cast our votes. We each have a white marble for yay and a black marble for nay. There is jar in the center of the kitchen counter where we will anonymously cast our votes. If there are any nays, the deal is a no-go, and no questions asked on who said nay."

Madge laughed and said, "I feel like we're electing a new pope and should send smoke signals up the chimney. But I think we need to open some wine first, and toast each other, and talk about holiday plans, and then cast our votes."

Trish and Suzy agreed that was a good idea to relieve some of the stress of this decision.

"So, Suzy, Tatiana told me she plans on coming back from Jamaica shortly after spending Christmas with her family to join Ian in Aspen for New Year's. Do you think this is getting serious?" Trish queried.

"They've been inseparable since Thanksgiving. And I haven't seen Ian this happy in a long time. She is such a lovely girl. I'm looking forward to getting to know her better."

"Yes, the sparks were definitely flying at Thanksgiving," added Madge. "And Suzy, I am glad you're all getting away. It seems like eons ago that I was the one who always spent Christmas in Aspen with some of my journalist friends. Now I can't imagine anyplace in the world I'd rather be than at the farm with Jason and our kids. Our lives have changed so much these past five years."

"Well, what will never change is our friendship and the love I have for the two of you—no matter what the marble vote," said Trish.

They all smiled in agreement.

"Okay, are we ready?" asked Suzy as she approached the jar. "Come cast your marble."

Suzy put her marble in last, then shook it three times for good measure and spilled out the marbles—three whites! They could barely contain their joy as they started hugging each other and leaping in the air.

Suzy opened the champagne and said, "Well, here's to The Three Tomatoes, and to my two best friends. Let's hope to hell we're doing the right thing."

CHAPTER 6

RINGING IN THE NEW

Vermont...

Madge awoke to the sensuous delight of soft kisses on her neck, and Jason's hand caressing her nipples. "Merry the day after Christmas."

Madge moaned, "Oh, this is lovely, but you know those two little hooligans will be pouncing on our bed any minute now."

"Not this morning. Mom and Dad already have them outside for sledding, so we can luxuriate right here in bed." Then his mouth slowly made its way farther down to her sweet spot. In no time, Madge urged him inside of her and they made exquisite, passionate love.

Satiated and sprawled out on the bed, Madge said with a throaty laugh, "Do you think your folks will take them sledding every morning this week?"

Jason laughed too, and then took the TV remote from the side of the bed, "Do you mind if I check out what's happening in the world?"

"Stay right there, and I'll bring up some coffee. There aren't many mornings we get to have coffee in bed and cuddle with the news like an old married couple," Madge laughed.

When she returned with two cups of piping hot coffee, she saw a stunned look on his face. "Jason, what's the matter?"

"Senator Sawyers died of a heart attack last night."

Madge was stunned too. Senator Sawyers was the longtime senior senator from New York and had been in office as long as Madge could remember. She had interviewed him many times over the years when she was in broadcast news. They both sat and watched the newscast in disbelief.

~~~~~~

Harlem...

Michael placed a cup of hot coffee on the bedstand for Trish and then went downstairs to retrieve *The New York Times* from the front steps of their brownstone. Michael still liked reading an actual paper and not one on a digital screen. He came back to the bedroom with the front page on display, with a bold headline, Senator Sawyers Dead. He and Trish poured over the article in shock.

They continued to discuss it over breakfast and what it would mean to New York, and who would be waiting in the wings to take his place.

"It will be interesting to see how this evolves. On another topic, just before I fell asleep last night, you said you had an idea to run by me," said Michael as he finished the last bite of the delicious omelet Trish had prepared.

"Well, now that Tatiana is in our lives, and I've had a chance to talk to her about her art and also had a chance to see the work of some of the other young artists at Parsons,
~~~~~~

it's really made me yearn for the art world again. So, I've been thinking...now that we're financially back on our feet, and with the up-front money coming in from The Three Tomatoes acquisition, I'd like to open a gallery again."

Michael sat there in silence until Trish finally said, "Michael, if you don't think it's a good idea, I won't even consider it."

But when Michael lifted his head, she saw a tear coming down his cheek. "Trish, I think it's a great idea. I have felt guilty for so long about destroying your dream and your beautiful art gallery in the Village by losing all our money when I had the hedge fund, and then my disastrous affair with Lacey that almost got you killed."

"Michael, that's all in the past."

"No wait, there's more I need to say. I know you love The Three Tomatoes and I have been so proud of how you pivoted your passion for health and wellness into creating that into an important part of The Three Tomatoes, but I know that art is really where your heart is," Michael said as he got up to embrace Trish. "You have my 1000 percent support. So, tell me what you're thinking, another gallery in the Village?"

"Actually, this time, I'm thinking it should be a gallery right here in the heart of Harlem. There's such a vibrant art community here already, and I'd love to showcase diversity in art in terms of race, gender, and of course artists of all ages."

"Well, the campus is closed until the end of January, so let's start scouting locations."

~~~~~~
~~~~~~

Aspen...

Suzy had headed back from the slopes to Margot's beautiful Aspen home early on New Year's Eve. She wanted to make the final preparations for the evening with Margot's wonderful cook and housekeeper, whom Margot had insisted be there for Suzy's holiday week. She was so grateful for that.

As she showered, she reflected on what a good decision it had been to spend the holidays here. She actually found herself laughing and enjoying life again without feeling guilty that Ken wasn't here to share those moments. The exhilaration of skiing down the slopes and feeling that Ken was nodding his approval went a long way in thawing the numbness since his death.

She wanted tonight to be lovely and special for all of them. On Christmas Day, Chris had proposed to Keri and presented her with a beautiful diamond ring. Keri was overjoyed. Chris was a solid, stable guy and he had been there for Keri in the worst moments of her life. She had a good feeling that theirs was a relationship that would weather the tests of time.

Tatiana had arrived two days earlier, and Ian was loving every second of teaching the "island girl" to ski.

She headed into the kitchen to talk to Margot's cook and help with the New Year's preparations. She was looking forward to the New Year.

CHAPTER 7
NEW DIRECTIONS

It was the second week into the New Year, and Trish, Madge, and Suzy had asked Amy, The Three Tomatoes CEO, to gather the staff so they could tell them about the acquisition and answer their questions. They had told Amy the day before and assured her she would remain as CEO.

The staff was understandably anxious and a little nervous with the news, but after Suzy explained why this would be good for the company's growth—explaining that each of them would get shares in the fastest growing streaming company in the world—and assured them their jobs were secure, everyone got excited.

An hour later they were comfortably seated at one of their favorite martini bars, clinking glasses, before their Ripe Tomatoes dinner. The sale of the company was so all encompassing since they returned after the New Year, they had barely had time to catch up with each other.

"That went better than I expected," said Suzy.

"I agree," said Madge. "And the fact that Amy, whom the

staff adores, is so enthusiastic really made a difference. So, enough about business, we need catch-up time. I'm so thrilled about Keri's engagement...tell us everything!"

"Well, Aspen was definitely the right place to spend the holidays. And of course, Keri and Chris had been talking about marriage, but she was truly surprised when he proposed on bended knee in front of Ian and me on Christmas Eve. He had called me the week before to ask my permission—such a sweet old-fashioned gesture. I didn't know when, but I was so glad he chose Christmas Eve. It turned the sadness we were all feeling into a joyous event."

"What about Ian and Tatiana?" Trish piped in.

"Tatiana is a pure delight. She fit in perfectly and Ian is gaga over her. And what did you and Michael do over the holidays?"

"Actually, I have news. I signed a lease on a storefront space in Harlem and I'm going to open another gallery." Trish went on to explain the details and her vision for a new gallery to the delight of Suzy and Madge.

"Trish, you don't know how happy that makes me. I feared you would never get over what happened in the gallery and had locked your love of art away with that terrible time."

Trish teared up a little. "You both saved me in those dark days, and it was seeing Tatiana's art that made me realize how much I was missing the art world."

"Well, there's certainly lots to catch up on at dinner tonight, so let's get going," said Suzy.

~~~~~~
~~~~~~

"You three never cease to amaze us," said Hope after hearing all their news. "Here's to much success moving ahead." They all had a champagne toast and good wishes.

"So, I have a little news too," said Hope after the toast. "I have a new producing partner, and we're raising money for a very exciting show." And then Hope, who always gave out every detail, uncharacteristically stopped there.

After they had waited in silence for Hope to continue, Arlene finally said, "Hope, are you going to keep us in suspense? We need details."

"Hold on to your Spanx, ladies, here comes the bombshell...my new partner is Ellen Martin."

There were gasps from around the table since Ellen had always been an archrival of Hope's and had pulled a lot of backstabbing moves that had hurt Hope over the years.

"Well, now that I've won a couple of Tonys, I don't feel so threatened by her anymore. So, when she invited me to lunch a few weeks ago, I went out of curiosity. She presented me with a literal olive branch, which was a great icebreaker. And then she told me she had acquired the rights to the best-selling biography about the legendary singer Whitney Jones and her tragic life, and wanted to turn it into a musical. But she knew she'd need a partner for this one and wanted to know if I'd be interested. I played it cool for a few days, but there was no way I was turning this down. So, there you have it. And mind you, it's all very confidential, so hush-hush."

While there were congratulations around the table, Suzy could sense the others shared her reservations about this partnership too.

The conversation then switched to the death of Senator Brian Sawyers. "What are you hearing about a replacement?"

asked Hope turning to Heather Stone who was chief White House correspondent at a major news network. In another irony of archrivals, Heather had once replaced Madge as the morning anchor of one of the top-rated network TV news shows, but they had become close friends over the years. Hope recently invited her to join the Ripe Tomatoes' dinners (since she was now over forty.)

"The way it works is that in the next few weeks, the governor will appoint someone to fill his seat and then there will be a special election for his senate seat this November. Of course, it's assumed the appointed person will be a candidate," Heather explained. "Right now, I'm hearing a lot of names being bandied around...and Madge, you didn't hear this from me, but one of those names I keep hearing is Jason Madison."

Madge laughed. "That's an interesting speculation, but the last person who would be interested in politics is Jason, although I think he is just what the senate needs."

~~~~~~

Five nights later, after the kids had gone to sleep, Jason poured their usual brandies and joined Madge by the fireplace. "I got a very unexpected call today from the governor. He wants to meet with me this week to discuss taking over the rest of Senator Sawyers's term."

"Well, I'll be damned," said Madge. "Heather mentioned the other night at dinner that your name was one of the ones she heard being bandied about, but I put it down to the rumor mills. What did you say?"

"I told him I was flattered, but that I'm not interested in politics. And he said that was precisely why he was reaching
~~~~~~

out to me because he thinks what we don't need in Washington right now is more political hacks. He finally convinced me to at least hear him out. I agreed to meet him the day after tomorrow."

Madge took a large swallow of brandy. "It is very flattering, and of course you should hear him out. I can't think of a better person than you to shake up the status quo, but I also know, having covered politics for many years, just how brutal it is."

"I hear you, and I have no intention of being in that jungle. It's just that he was so insistent that I hear him out, I agreed. I will listen politely and then say no."

CHAPTER 8
OFF AND RUNNING

It was a bitter cold February evening and Suzy was grateful that Madge and Trish hadn't backed out of having dinner in her new apartment. She had ordered in from one of their favorite Italian restaurants, and she had the martini shaker at the ready for their first toast.

"It's colder than a witch's tit," said Madge as she entered the foyer and kissed Suzy on the cheek.

"A martini will warm you up. Trish is already here, and we were just waiting for you to pour the martinis."

Madge walked into the living room and joined Trish who was looking at the spectacular view from Suzy's windows. It was one of those rare crystal clear nights in Manhattan.

"Beautiful, isn't it?" Trish said to Madge as Suzy walked in with the tray of martinis.

They each lifted a glass and gently clinked. "Here's to a new life for you, Suzy, in your beautiful new home."

They then curled up on the overstuffed sectional couch and started to catch up on everything that had transpired since the start of the New Year. The Three Tomatoes was now officially part of North Star Entertainment, and Trish was planning a spring opening of her gallery. But the big news this evening was from Madge.

"Well, ladies, I can't believe this is actually happening, but I wanted you to be the first to know—the governor is announcing tomorrow that he is appointing Jason as our interim senator."

"That's huge news and so exciting," said Suzy.

"Senator Madison...now that has quite the ring. And Jason is just the kind of person we need in Washington," Trish chimed in.

When Madge didn't respond right away, Suzy asked, "How are you feeling about all this?"

"To be honest, I have mixed feelings, and I think Jason does too. On the one hand, he is one of the smartest and most honorable people around, and he really cares about the important issues. I know he will be a great senator. But I also know how private he is, and this will really put him and our family out there. And you know, since he sold Snazzed and the children came along, he has devoted himself to being there for them. Just between us, I am concerned about how this will change our lives if he decides to run in November, and then if he actually wins. Does that sound selfish?"

"Not at all," said Trish, and Suzy nodded in agreement.

"We will just have to see how it all plays out."

Over dinner, Trish caught them up on the gallery news and her plans to open with her first show in the spring. "And, Suzy, don't mention this to Ian yet, but I want to include some of Tatiana's paintings. I'm meeting her at the gallery this week to show her the space and then I will tell her I'd love to include some of her work."

"Oh, that is wonderful, Trish. I'm sure she will be thrilled."

Then Madge and Trish turned to Suzy for an update on how things were going at The Three Tomatoes.

"Amy and I have a meeting coming up with the head of marketing at North Star. They want to talk about marketing ideas for promoting The Three Tomatoes and they have a hefty promotion budget, so this should be exciting. I'll let you know how it goes."

At the end of the meal, Suzy poured them all a wonderful port, and then raised her glass, saying, "To the two best friends in the world and to our continued adventures."

~~~~~~

Madge knew it would be a media frenzy, and it was. But she was really taken with how gracefully Jason answered the reporters' questions. As they threw questions at Madge, she tried to play the smiling politician's wife so that the spotlight would stay on Jason, but it wasn't easy. This was, after all, a room full of journalists who still thought of Madge as the hard-core journalist she had once been.

That night, as they lay in bed, Jason asked with his arms wrapped around her, "Hon, am I doing the right thing? I love you and the kids more than anything in the world, but I feel called to do this. And hell, I haven't even figured out how I'll deal with all the back and forth between DC and New York."

Madge sat up. "Jason, listen to me. This is a chance for you to make a difference in ways that you haven't been able to do before now. I couldn't be prouder of you. You have supported me in everything I've wanted to do—from the documentaries, adopting the children, and being here for them when I've been
~~~~~~

pursuing my dreams, so now it's my turn to support you in doing this. We'll figure it out together."

Jason pulled her back into his arms, and gave her a long deep kiss. And then they both fell asleep almost instantly.

~~~~~~

Trish was standing in the middle of the space that would soon be her new gallery and envisioning the opening night reception when Tatiana walked through the front door.

"I am so glad you could join me here," Trish greeted her with a hug.

Tatiana looked around, taking it all in. "This is a wonderful space, and you are so lucky to have found something in the heart of 125th Street. How did you find this?"

"It was serendipity. I happened to run into a wonderful artist whose work I featured early in his career and we grabbed a cup coffee to catch up. When I mentioned I was thinking of opening another gallery, he told me about his friend who owned a gallery and was ready to retire. So, here I am, in this beautiful space with a wonderful local history too."

"I, for one, can't wait to be at the opening reception." Tatiana beamed.

"I certainly hope so, because I plan on exhibiting some of your beautiful pieces."

It took a couple of minutes for Trish's words to sink in and then Tatiana grabbed Trish's hands all the while saying, "Oh my God, oh my God, oh my God."

"It's only fitting that my last exhibit was your aunt's final work, and your work will be among the first in my new gallery. It's a brand-new beginning."
~~~~~~

~~~~~~

Tatiana had waited all day to tell Ian. It was Valentine's Day and they were having dinner at the most romantic restaurant in New York City, One If by Land.

As they took their first sips of champagne, Tatiana told him the exciting news.

"Babe, I'm so happy for you. You're beautiful, talented, and the most amazing girl I've ever met," Ian gushed.

"You're not so bad yourself," she laughed. "And this is the most beautiful restaurant." Just then there was a bit of commotion and they both turned around, as did several other diners, to see a young man on his knees proposing to his date.

"Oh, I should have mentioned. This romantic restaurant is the scene of many engagements. Who knows, maybe one..."

Before he could finish the thought, she shushed him.

"I'm sorry, Tatiana. I don't mean to be rushing you. We have lots of time, but I just want you to know how much you mean to me."

"And you mean a great deal to me too, Ian. You've made these past few months in New York City so magical."

"Let's keep making them magical."

Tatiana smiled, but in her heart, she wasn't sure that could happen. And the last thing she ever wanted to do was to break Ian's heart.
~~~~~~

CHAPTER 9
COURSE CORRECTION

It was late March, and after a brutally cold winter, the day was a wonderful reminder that spring was around the corner. It was almost sixty degrees and New Yorkers were strolling the streets without winter coats and taking their time instead of their usual head-on rush.

Suzy and Amy didn't have time for spring fever as they headed up in the elevator to the executive offices of North Star Entertainment for a meeting with the head of marketing. They were ushered into a beautiful conference room on one of the upper floors of the Freedom Tower, where they were greeted enthusiastically by Jesse Middleton, the chief marketing officer.

"Suzy and Amy, great to see you both again. The ad agency will be here any moment to present some of their ideas for the new marketing campaign."

"We're excited. Amy and I were just saying it will be interesting to be on the other side of the conference table with an agency presenting to us."

"Oh, that's right," said Jesse. "I almost forgot you both

came out of the ad agency business. Your input will be even more valuable."

North Star's ad agency was part of one of the largest agency networks in the world. When the team arrived, Suzy was pleasantly surprised to see that Bill Stanton, one of the top executives, was with them. Bill and Suzy had worked together several years prior at another agency as young account executives.

"Suzy, you never change," Bill greeted her with a warm smile and a hug.

Suzy was impressed that Bill was joining them for a meeting that would typically be handled by the account team. As she looked at Bill, she had to admit middle age had only made him even more handsome, with his graying hair at his temples and gentle smile lines around his eyes.

They settled in at the conference table and the agency started off by presenting a beautiful animated logo for The Three Tomatoes that moved out from the North Star logo. Amy, who was a former agency creative director, loved it, as did Suzy.

It wasn't until they got to some of the creative concepts and then the media plan that Suzy started to get a sinking feeling. All the ads featured women who looked like they were in their late twenties to midthirties. And while it was exciting to see a media budget that was in the millions, the media being proposed was not The Three Tomatoes's demographic of women forty-five-plus.

Suzy looked around the room, and then it hit her. Aside from Amy and Bill, everyone in the room was in their twenties and thirties. She had a sudden flashback to the last agency she had worked for, Secret Agent, and her "twelve-year-old boss" who fired her. That turned out to be the best thing that ever happened to her since it was the catalyst to start The Three Tomatoes. But it was still traumatic.

Jesse had been enthusiastically nodding throughout the entire presentation, and then turned to Amy and Suzy. "What do you think?"

Suzy deferred to Amy as she tried to keep her own emotions in check.

"There are many elements of the creative that are wonderful. I especially love the animated logo. And I know these are concepts, but the images feel more thirtysomething than forty- or even fiftysomething."

Suzy had composed herself enough to pipe in. "I agree with Amy that there are some clever creative ideas, but like the images, some of the media suggestions also seem to be geared to a younger audience. As you know, our demographic is upscale, well-educated women who are over forty-five...they want to be able to see themselves in these images. And I don't think they're consuming some of the media you've suggested."

With that, the thirtysomething media director from the agency responded that Jesse's brief to them was to broaden the demo to include a younger audience, which was admittedly a tricky balance between the older demographic.

Suzy looked over at Jesse with raised eyebrows and said as sweetly as she could, "Jesse, I think we should review the briefs you gave to the agency after this meeting to make sure we're all on the same page with the target audience."

Jesse squirmed uncomfortably. "Oh, of course." He then turned to the agency team and thanked them for all the time they had put into the initial presentation. "After Amy and Suzy and I have a chance to review and discuss, I'll get back to you with our feedback."

Amy and Suzy thanked the team as well. As Bill was leaving, he said quietly to Suzy that he'd give her a call.

As soon as the agency had cleared the room, Suzy turned to Jesse. "I'm confused. What's going on here? You do know that our core audience is midlife-and-beyond women?"

"Well, yes, of course, Suzy. And that's a very important demo. But your subscriber base is stagnant right now, and we really think broadening your appeal to a slightly younger market, and especially the young mom audience who will evolve into your core demo, is a growth opportunity."

While Suzy sat there a bit stunned, Amy chimed in. "Jesse, while certainly some of our content appeals to women of any age, it definitely skews to older women, so I think targeting an audience that will be disappointed once they get the product will just turn them off."

"I'm glad you brought that up, Amy. We were thinking you might want to revamp some of your content to appeal to parenting and fertility issues, for example."

"And who is the 'we' in this conversation?" asked Suzy, a little more sharply than she had intended.

"Our marketing team was looking at ways to grow subscribers. It was just one of the thoughts we came up with," Jesse stammered, realizing he just might have royally pissed off Suzy.

"May I suggest the next time your marketing team convenes, and before you brief the agency, that you include our marketing team who intimately knows and understands our demographic."

"Of course, of course. My apologies to both of you. Like all new relationships it will just take a little while to get to know each other," he said with his most ingratiating smile.

"You're very right, Jesse. And we are definitely excited about launching a new campaign to grow subscribers and with an incredible media budget too. May I suggest that you and Amy schedule a meeting soon in our offices with your team and ours, so everyone gets on the same page?"

"Absolutely," said Jesse with his still pasted-on smile as he escorted them to the elevator.

They waited until they were on the street before Amy turned to Suzy, exclaiming, "WTF?"

"I know, Amy. Let's just hope it's a bump in the road and we can course-correct."

~~~~~~

Later that afternoon Suzy got a call from Bill Stanton.

"Suzy, it was great seeing you today. I am in awe of what you have created with The Three Tomatoes. And I have to say I'm embarrassed that the agency was so obviously offtrack today."

"Oh, Bill, it was definitely not the agency's fault. The briefing from Jesse's team was clearly off the mark, but I think we'll have that righted soon. I really appreciated that you took the time to be there today."

"Well, to be honest, I wanted a chance to see you again. It's been a long time. So, how about I buy you dinner soon and we catch up?"

Suzy paused for a moment, and then to her own surprise, found herself agreeing to meet for dinner the following week.
~~~~~~

CHAPTER 10

BACK IN THE GAME

"One hour to opening," Trish said excitedly and a little anxiously too. "Have we forgotten anything?"

"It's going to be an incredible evening, and everything looks perfect. Almost as perfect as the two of you," said Michael as he put an arm around Trish and Tatiana.

"I'm so nervous, I'm shaking," said Tatiana.

"I have just what you both need to relax." He was back in seconds with a glass of champagne for each of them. "Here's to a wonderful opening night."

"And here's to both of you," said Trish. "Tatiana, I don't know what I would have done without all your help these past few weeks. Especially for all the effort you put into getting the word out on social media. People are going to love your work and they will be so excited to meet you."

"Thank you, Trish. I don't have the words to express how grateful I am to you."

"It looks like you'll get some great press here tonight too," added Michael.

"Well, I suspect some of that might be because they're hoping our new Senator Madison will be attending. Just so long as they mention us too, I'll be happy."

By 7:00 p.m. the gallery could not fit another person. It was a who's who of the art world, the theater world (thanks to Hope), New York society (thanks to Celeste), Harlem's community and business leaders (thanks to Michael), and the media, who all wanted a quote or two from Jason.

Ian could not take his eyes off Tatiana. She was wearing a simple cream-colored sheath that looked beautiful next to her glowing brown skin. Her hair was braided on the top of her head in a crown and with her graceful movements, she a was a regal queen. He loved watching her talk to her admirers who were as much in awe of her as they were of her art.

"She's really special," Suzy said coming alongside her son. A moment later, they were joined by Bill Stanton, who handed Suzy a glass of wine.

"Bill, this is my son, Ian. Ian, Bill and I worked together many years ago and his agency is now handling The Three Tomatoes."

Ian and Bill shook hands and exchanged greetings. *So, this is the guy Mom's had a couple of dinners with that she says weren't dates,* thought Ian. *Mom might not think they're dates, but it's obvious by the way Bill is looking at her that he certainly does.* But his mom looked beautiful tonight and actually seemed happy.

There was an audible buzz, and Suzy looked toward the door to see the arrival of Jason and Madge, who were immediately surrounded by press. They politely made their way through the press and well-wishers to hug and congratulate Trish.

Madge whispered in Trish's ear, "I'm sorry for the fucking madhouse we've created."

Trish whispered back, "As long as they mention the name of the gallery," and they both laughed.

By nine o'clock the last of the guests had left, leaving just Trish, Michael, Tatiana, Ian, Suzy, and Bill. Madge had given her apologies because Jason wanted to get home to see the children to bed.

"This was a spectacular evening, Trish," said Suzy, lifting her champagne glass. "And Tatiana, I would say you have now been officially launched into the New York City art world. Cheers to both of you."

"Michael and I made reservations at Red Rooster Harlem...can you all join us?" asked Trish.

Tatiana and Ian begged off. It was Ian's last week of law school and graduation was in two weeks.

"I'd love to join you," said Suzy. "Bill, what about you?"

"As delightful as that sounds, I have an early flight to the West Coast, but I hope there's a rain check here." He wished Trish much success with the gallery.

Suzy walked him to the door. "Thanks for being here tonight."

"There was no place else I'd rather be. I'll be back in New York on Friday. Are you free for dinner Saturday night?"

"That sounds lovely," said Suzy. He gave her a hug and kiss on the cheek and headed out the door.

~~~~~~

"As beautiful as you looked in that sexy dress tonight, I couldn't wait to get it off you," Ian said as he caressed Tatiana's beau-
~~~~~~

tiful body, after they had made love for the second time that night, with a fervor that's unrivaled with young lovers. "Do you really have to go home for the summer?"

Tatiana sighed. She had dreaded telling Ian she had to go back home for a while, and it would be even more difficult leaving him. But she knew she had to deal with things at home if she was ever going to have a chance of being with Ian.

"Oh, Ian, you know I must. But I promised you I would stay to see you graduate from law school next weekend, and to celebrate that occasion. Please don't make it harder for me to say goodbye. It's only until September."

Ian gave her a deep passionate kiss. "It will be a long cold summer without you, babe."

~~~~~~

Trish, Michael, and Suzy were settled into a cozy booth in the back of Red Rooster Harlem. It had been great to relax and rehash the evening, which had been quite a success. Trish felt she was finally back in the art game.

"I'd forgotten how much I love this place," said Suzy. "It's the best fried chicken on the planet."

"Oh God, yes," said Trish as she licked one of her fingers. "And it's dangerously close to the gallery. I just wish your friend Bill had joined us."

Michael gave her that *don't start prying* look.

Suzy laughed. "Okay, Trish, I know you've been dying to ask all evening. We've gone out a few times. At first it was just catching up with an old friend, and a little business too because we are a client of his agency. But if I'm honest with myself, I guess we are sort of dating now."
~~~~~~

"He seems like a nice guy. What's his story?"

"He was definitely a player when we were young, and then he married the boss's daughter. He quickly rose up the ranks of the agency, which many attributed to nepotism, but I have to say he is one of the best account guys in the business. He's charming and clients love him, so I think he would have made it to the top in any event. They divorced a few years ago. I do enjoy being around him, and it's nice to have someone to go out to dinner with, but I'm really not ready for a relationship."

"Okay, I think that's enough of an interrogation for tonight," said Michael jokingly. "Listen, Suzy, you'll know when you're ready. You don't have to rush into anything. Just enjoy being happy for a while and see where it takes you."

"Well, what would really make me happy right now is Chef Samuelsson's rum chocolate cake," laughed Suzy.

CHAPTER 11

THE PAST RETURNS

It was a rainy, dreary day that felt more like early April than the middle of May. The raw, damp wind coming off the Great Peconic Bay sent a chill through Suzy as she stood at the gravesite of her great aunt, Millie O'Brien. She was glad that Ian had joined her, since they were the last of Aunt Millie's family. Suzy was heartened to see so many townspeople had shown up to pay their respects. At ninety-two, most of her aunt's contemporaries were long gone, but the O'Brien family had been a mainstay on the North Fork of Long Island for nearly three hundred years.

Aunt Millie was her mother's aunt, and when Suzy was growing up, they had spent many glorious summers at "the farm." Located on fifty acres in Jamesport, including land that was adjacent to the Peconic Bay, it was a heavenly place for kids and grown-ups alike.

The farm had originally been one of the many potato farms that dotted the eastern end of Long Island, now known as the North Fork. Many of these farms became vineyards starting in the early 1970s when a few enterprising locals realized the soil was very much like that of France's and Italy's. With over thirty vineyards producing world-class wine the sleepy North Fork had become a popular tourist destination. But unlike the celebrity and hedge fund conspicuous consumption-laden Hamptons, the North Fork was much more laid-back, with tiny hamlets that were still home to families that had lived there for generations.

Aunt Millie was one of those, and while she had received many lucrative offers over the years to sell off some of her fifty acres to vineyards, she adamantly refused, although she did lease some of the land to local farmers. The farmhouse was sadly run-down. Suzy's parents had tried for years to get Aunt Millie to make repairs that they would have paid for, but she refused. After they died, Suzy tried her best to convince Aunt Millie to sell the property and get something smaller in town. But she was stubborn, and the best Suzy could do was to insist that she get a live-in housekeeper, which she finally agreed to.

At Suzy's invitation, the pastor had invited all the guests in the church to a luncheon at one of the many charming inns in the area. She made her way around the tables greeting people she had little or no memory of, but who knew her late aunt and her family. Occasionally there was someone she had played with as a child during the summers at the farm, many of whom had settled there.

It was getting toward the end of the luncheon and people were saying their goodbyes and last condolences when she heard her name spoken in that unmistakable voice. She knew this day would come, but she had not expected it to be this day.

"Suzy," he said again, as she slowly turned around.

And there he was. Devon Gerrity. It had been thirty-seven

years, and his face was now that of a middle-aged man, but his hair was still ginger, and even with his beard, she would have recognized him anywhere.

"Devon, how thoughtful of you to come."

"Well, I was just about to tell you who I am. A man changes a lot over the years, so I'm glad you recognized me. But, Suzy, you look like time has stood still."

She suddenly found herself embarrassingly blushing, and her heart was inexplicably racing. She was relieved when Ian appeared.

"Devon, meet my son, Ian."

As they shook hands, Devon said, "Nice to meet you, Ian. I'm a childhood friend of your mother, and I knew your aunt Millie. She was a firecracker. I'm sorry for your loss."

"Are you staying around long?" he said addressing Suzy.

"Just for a few days," Suzy responded, not wanting to look in those still very green eyes. "I need to meet with Aunt Millie's lawyer and straighten a few things out."

"Maybe you'll have time for a cup of coffee before you leave? It would be nice to catch up. Are you staying at the farm?"

"Yes, we are, but it's going to be a hectic few days and then I need to get back to New York City."

He looked disappointed. "Well, good seeing you, Suzy, and nice to meet you, Ian."

~~~~~~

Suzy and Ian had decided to stay at the farm. Suzy was glad that Maddy, the housekeeper, had agreed to stay on and help with anything they needed. She had made up two of the guest
~~~~~~

rooms and had a hot pot of tea waiting when they returned.

"So, Mom, what are you going to do with this place?"

"Let's see what happens at the lawyer's office tomorrow when he reads us the will. Aunt Millie always said she was leaving the place to me. I'll probably put it up for sale, but honestly, look around this house. It will most likely be a teardown."

"That would be so sad, Mom. Sure, it needs work, but it has a lot of charm, and so much history too."

"We'll see, but I just don't think I have the energy to even think about renovating a place like this."

~~~~~~

Suzy and Ian headed into town first thing in the morning to Mitch Adams's law office. He was third generation, and his father had originally been Aunt Millie's lawyer.

"Suzy, as I am sure you expected, your aunt has left everything to you, which mostly includes the farmhouse and the property."

"Yes, she told me after my parents died that she was leaving everything to me."

"There is one condition she may not have mentioned to you...and it's a big one. I think it's just easier if I read you the letter."

Dear Suzy,

It is my dearest wish for you to have the farm and the land that has been in our family for three hundred years. My great desire would be for you to keep the farm and the land in the family. But I know that times have changed, and I will
~~~~~~

understand if you want to sell it, but with one proviso. You must NEVER sell it to one of those greedy corporations who are buying all our land and turning them into vineyard after vineyard with no soul or sense of our community. If you cannot abide by this request, then I will leave it to the park, and they can turn it into a nature preserve.

Your Loving Aunt Millie

Suzy sat back, a bit shocked. "Well, I knew she wasn't happy with all the vineyards, but that's where the value of the land is. And I would never sell it to a developer who would turn it into town houses that are popping up everywhere."

"You're right, Suzy. I tried to talk her out of this, but she was adamant. I know the house and the land are a lot to take on."

"I'll need time to digest all of this. We might just be better off giving the land to the park."

"Whatever your decision is, Suzy, I'll be here to help."

"Thanks, Mitch."

Ian hadn't said a word until they were in the car heading back to the farm. "Mom, you can't sell it or give it away. It's our heritage."

"I know, Ian, but with everything going on with The Three Tomatoes, and your dad's death, I just don't think I can deal with this."

As they pulled up to the farmhouse, there was a pickup truck parked outside, and who was standing there but Devon.

"Hey, Suzy. Sorry to drop in, but I thought I'd bring the coffee to you and maybe you'd give us a few minutes to catch up?" He held up a large thermos of coffee he had brought with him.

Damn him. He can still make me feel like I'm a googly-eyed sixteen-year-old. "All right, Devon, have a seat on the porch and I'll bring out the mugs."

Suzy returned and they cheered with their coffee mugs.

"It's good to see you, Suzy. I was sorry to hear about your husband, and now of course your aunt. I know she never liked me much, but I always admired her. She'll be missed around here."

"So, tell me about you, Devon, and your vineyard. And how is Carol?"

"We divorced about five years ago. But we still own the vineyard together, so it's good it was an amicable split. Actually, the vineyard is one of the things I was hoping to talk to you about. We're looking to expand, and we'd make you a fair offer on any of your acres here if you're thinking of selling."

"Devon, my aunt just died," she said with an edge. "I'm not sure what I'm doing with this place yet, but I can assure you I won't be selling any acres to you."

Devon looked a little taken aback. "Oh God, Suzy, forgive me. Believe me, I wasn't trying to take advantage of the situation. And I really wanted to see you and catch up on your life... it's been a long time. Is Ian your only child? He seems like a terrific young man."

Suzy softened a little. "I also have a daughter. She recently got engaged and Ian just finished law school. They're great kids and I'm fortunate."

"I always wanted kids, especially a son, but it just wasn't in the cards," he said wistfully.

Suzy felt a sudden pit in her stomach. "Devon, I hope you'll excuse me, but I'm only here for a couple of days and I have a lot to get done. It was good catching up," she said as she reached out her hand for an awkward handshake, and then headed into the house.

CHAPTER 12

NEVER GIVE UP ON LOVE

Suzy, Madge, and Trish were enjoying sitting on the sidewalk patio of Red Rooster Harlem, each with a martini in hand. This had become their new favorite meetup place and they had even convinced the Ripe Tomatoes to have their dinner here tonight, rather than their usual Midtown haunt.

"First things first," said Trish. "Catch us up on the latest with The Three Tomatoes and North Star. The ad campaign is beautiful and thank goodness it features age-appropriate women."

"Yes, our first skirmish. It took Bill Stanton stepping in though to make the case to Matt Greene over eighteen holes of golf. You know, the old boys club at work. I would have had no problem marching into Matt's office, but I suppose having Bill say something was a better approach. The bottom line will be if the campaign helps to increase subscribers."

"Speaking of Bill, what's the story? You seem to be spending a lot of time together and curious minds want to know if you finally did the deed."

"Madge!" exclaimed a horrified Trish.

"Oh, it's all right," laughed Suzy. "He's a really nice guy and I enjoy his company. But I'm not ready for the next step. Maybe I'm still numb when it comes to feeling passion again."

"Well, maybe with time you'll feel that again," said Trish, always the optimist.

"In my experience," said Madge, "and I've had considerably more in that department than both of you, it's either there or it's not. So, tell us, what have you decided to do about your aunt's farm?"

"That's my other news. Ian is passionate about keeping the farm. He was supposed to start working in Ken's law firm this month, but he decided he'd like to postpone that to the fall and take on the renovation of the farmhouse. He also said it will help take his mind off how much he's missing Tatiana this summer. After several long discussions, I agreed. I just hope it's the right decision. But enough about me. Madge, tell us how things are going with Jason. It must be quite an adjustment for all of you."

"It's a little bit of everything right now. There is something very exciting about politics. The first time I sat in the senate gallery and saw Jason with his Senator Madison nameplate in front of him it was an extraordinary moment. But it's definitely a big change at home with Jason gone a great deal of the time. The kids miss him, and he misses them.

"The best thing we did though was to invite Bertha to live in with us in Brooklyn. We weren't sure she'd leave Vermont, and we were so happy she said yes. She adores the children, and they adore her. And you know she use to babysit Jason when she was in high school. So, that's working out, which is a good thing because now we have to start to think about Jason's campaign, and I want to help all I can."

"You know we're with you," said Trish. "I'm happy to host some events for Jason at the gallery too."

Just then, Hope appeared with some of the other Ripe Tomatoes who had shared an Uber uptown. "There's the beautiful trio. And I need one of those martinis pronto—I rarely venture out of Broadway and Times Square so this is quite the escapade."

They were soon seated inside at a round table tucked away in the back of the restaurant, and were delighted by the very charming Chef Samuelsson who personally greeted them.

Over martinis, wine, and fried chicken, they went around the table catching up.

They all wanted to know how Hope and Ellen were getting along as coproducers of the new musical that was coming to Broadway in the fall.

"The good news is by partnering, we were able to raise money in record time. I guess investors believe that our combined individual track records with successful shows will be a big plus for this one. Things were going fine until this week. Ellen is grousing about the director—she thinks he's out of his league with this show. But I saw his genius when he directed *If Tomorrow Never Comes* and got us a Tony, so we may butt heads on this."

Arlene, a former fashion and beauty editor, who was now an editorial consultant at The Three Tomatoes, shared some of her humorous dating disaster stories.

Madge laughed as she reminded the group that she used to be the one with the disastrous dates.

When Arlene's husband died of Alzheimer's two years ago, after being in a memory care facility for four years, she finally decided it was time to find some companionship. "It's really not easy at my age. I don't want to end up being someone's caretaker again and it seems the only guys interested in me are looking for just that."

Celeste chimed in. "You must never give up on finding love because when you least expect it, that is when it will find you. Look at me." She was a great example, having found love again in her seventies with one of the top mystery writers in the world, a dashing Englishman no less. And now they split their time between his estate outside London and her New York City apartment.

"Well, you are that shining example of Cinderella finding her prince in her seventies, and you didn't even have to lose a shoe," pronounced Hope, and they all laughed.

They continued to go around the table, laughing and sharing their stories. Trish looked around in awe at this wonderful group of accomplished women who could still turn heads, even the ones in their seventies, and who were so supportive of each other. As they were finishing their coffees and after-dinner drinks, Trish raised her glass. "Here's to the Ripe Tomatoes. Thank you all for heading uptown tonight. And you see, Hope? You didn't even need a passport." They all laughed the way that only dear friends can.

~~~~~~

Suzy had just taken her first sip of morning coffee when her cell phone rang, and Hope's name flashed on her screen. *Something's wrong for Hope to call this early.*

She barely said hello when Hope started shouting hysterically, "Have you seen what that bitch did? I knew I never should have partnered with her. She's a Botox-filled two-faced
~~~~~~

backstabber."

"Hope, calm down a little. What are you talking about?"

"Go to Page Six right now—her treachery is there in black and white."

Suzy opened the browser on her phone and went to Page Six and there was the story. *The backstage claws have come out on the set of the new musical about the life of the legendary Whitney Jones that Hope Allen and Ellen Martin are coproducing. Sources say that Allen wants the director out and Martin is standing firm that he stays. Insiders aren't surprised that this old rivalry has reared its ugly head.*

"Hope, you said it was Ellen who wanted to get rid of the director."

"Exactly. He just called me and quit...he said he couldn't believe after we won a Tony together that I would do this to him, and that he had to read it in Page Six."

"Well, where would they have gotten this story?"

"Oh, Suzy, you are so naive. Obviously, Ellen planted the story, and it was her way of getting rid of the director and making me look bad to boot."

"You don't actually know that, Hope...maybe you should give Ellen a chance to explain how this twisted story got out."

"You're damned right she's going to explain. I'm headed to her apartment right now."

"Hope, my only suggestion would be that you calm down a bit before you confront her. Maybe someone else is spreading rumors." But before Suzy could finish this last sentence Hope had said a hurried goodbye.

Suzy loved Hope dearly, but she was a drama queen. But then again so was Ellen. *It will be interesting to see how this partnership plays out*, Suzy mused.

She finished her coffee and was thinking about the long Memorial Day weekend. She was heading out to Jamesport to meet with Ian and look over the renovation plans he had just received from the architect. It was great to see him so excited about this project and she was glad to have an excuse not to spend the weekend with Bill at his summer place in Sag Harbor.

He was disappointed, but she had agreed to join him for a sail on Saturday since his fifty-foot sailboat was docked nearby in Greenport. He had invited a few of his friends, and Suzy asked him if Arlene could join them. She had a home in Sag Harbor too, and Bill had agreed to pick her up and drive her to Greenport.

Maybe when they got back to New York, it would be time to have the conversation she'd been wanting to have with him for a while. She enjoyed his company, and liked him as a friend, but this relationship wasn't going anywhere beyond that, and she thought they both knew that.

CHAPTER 13

CHANCE MEETINGS

Madge had been looking forward to the long weekend all month and spending three glorious days with Jason and the children in Vermont, away from all the political madness. She and Bertha and the kids had driven up on Thursday and Jason arrived that night from DC.

She let the children stay up past their bedtime so they could see their dad.

"Daddy, Daddy, I lost a tooth this week," Bitania blurted out the second Jason walked in the door.

"Well, I hope the tooth fairy made a visit, for your very first tooth," he said as he swept her up in his arms.

Yonas was right behind, saying, "Dad, Dad, I need you to help me practice my batting tomorrow."

"All right, kids," said Madge. "Let Dad at least sit down first before you catch him up on your week." She looked over at Jason who was in his glory with the kids, and said, "I'll bring you a glass of wine."

An hour later, Jason had tucked the kids in bed, and returned to the cozy living room to join Madge. "Well, now I can catch up on your week," he said as he pulled Madge in close for a kiss.

She caught him up on the latest family's and friend's news, including Suzy's news about keeping the farm and Ian's plans to stay out East and renovate the farmhouse, and postpone joining his dad's old law firm.

"You know I'm actually glad to hear that. Ian told me at Thanksgiving that he had reservations about following his father's footsteps into corporate law. I'm glad he's giving himself some time to figure things out."

"There's that, and the fact that he's barely heard from Tatiana since she returned home to Jamaica, so it's good for him to have other things to focus on," added Madge.

"I'm just so happy to have the next three days with you and the kids here, before the campaigning gets wound up," said Jason.

"Speaking of that, I think Heather's suggestion to think about Lindsey Campbell as your campaign manager is a good one. She has excellent credentials, and she is gung ho on your platform, especially around women's issues. I scheduled a meeting for you with her on Tuesday."

"You know I trust your instincts, Madge, so if you're impressed with Lindsey, I know I will be too. The rumor mill has it that State Senator Frank Delano will be my opponent. He has a lot of support in Albany and knows how to work the machine, so I could be in for a tough race."

"Jason," Madge purred, "he won't stand a chance, not when every woman in the entire state of New York wishes she was cuddled up right here next to you."

"Honey, much as I appreciate that endorsement, I think it's going to take a little more than sex appeal to win this election."

~~~~~~

Suzy went over the architect's plans with Ian and loved what she saw, and especially Ian's enthusiasm.

"You see, Mom, the basic structure of the house is still in great shape. What it's been lacking is tender loving care, and a vision of what it can be. We can start with the repair work...a new roof and rebuilding the wraparound porch, and then move on to the bigger things. We definitely need a new kitchen, and taking down some of the walls to make that part of a great room will make a big difference in the feel of house. We'll add some picture windows to take advantage of the landscape views, and then eventually we can upgrade the bathrooms. By next summer it will be a totally new place."

"I love it, but that's going to take someone to be here to oversee the renovations and make sure everything goes the way it's supposed to, and you're starting your new job right after Labor Day."

"Well, about that. I know how much Dad wanted me to join the firm with him, and I wanted to honor that, but a big corporate law firm just doesn't feel like the right thing for me. But I don't want you to be disappointed in me."

Suzy got up and put her arms around him. "Ian, you could never disappoint me. And you could never have disappointed Dad. He, of all people, would have told you to follow your own path."

"Thanks for saying that, Mom. Actually, I've had a couple of conversations with Mitch Adams. He's been looking for a young lawyer to join him. I like that it's a small local firm, and they do just about everything, from wills to working with
~~~~~~

some of the local vineyards. He said I could start this summer, and after I take the bar exam in the fall, he'd welcome me as a junior partner. I really like it out here, and this way I'd be here to oversee all the work on the house. I think Tatiana will be impressed that there are a lot of artists out here, and galleries too."

"Oh, honey, that's a wonderful plan. And how is Tatiana?"

"I'm not sure, Mom. We only talk a couple of times a week and she's very evasive when I ask questions. She just says she has some family things to work out. I don't want to push her, but it makes me nervous."

"I think you're right not to push her now. I'm sure she'll tell you what's going on when she's ready."

~~~~~~

Saturday was a perfect day for sailing. Suzy was glad she had joined Bill and his friends, and she was so happy to have Arlene there too.

Bill was at the helm with one of his buddies. Suzy and Arlene were enjoying a glass of champagne, the wind, and the sun from the stern.

"There's something about being out on the water that takes all your cares away," said Suzy.

"I agree. You know my husband and I had a sailboat for years, and it's one of the things I've really missed," said Arlene. "Of course, ours wasn't quite as big or luxurious as this one. You're lucky to have found a guy like Bill."

"He's not my guy, Arlene. We knew each other a lot of years ago. He's charming, and fun, and nice to be around, and I have to say he was a big step in my moving forward. I'm
~~~~~~

grateful for that, but I've realized lately that this is never going to develop into a real relationship, not that I'm ready for one. In fact, when we get back to New York next week, I was planning to have that conversation with him."

"Oh really?" said Arlene. Suzy couldn't help noticing how Arlene's glance went toward Bill, who looked every inch the debonair captain.

They docked the boat back in Greenport at five o'clock. "Suzy, are you sure you don't want to come back to Sag Harbor with us for dinner? You can stay the night, or I'll send you back to Jamesport in an Uber," said Bill, taking her aside.

"As lovely as that sounds, I have plans with Ian." This was a little white lie, since Ian had told her he had plans with some friends from the city who were visiting the vineyards. "But thank you for a perfectly delightful day. Thanks for bringing Arlene out too. You should get to know her better—she's an avid sailor like you." With that she gave him a hug and a kiss on the cheek.

She decided to walk around the docks a bit and admire the yachts. It was a beautiful day and as she walked past Claudio's, an excellent seafood place right on the dock, she decided to stop and have a glass of wine. There were several outdoor tables available. She was seated at a table for two and ordered a glass of chardonnay.

"Well, I hope that's one of ours," said the voice that she still heard in her head all these years later.

"Oh, Devon, hello."

"Are you expecting someone? If not, how about I join you?"

Damn, the man looked gorgeous. He was wearing cargo shorts, boat shoes, and a shirt with his vineyard's name on it. She could see his muscles bulging under the shirt, and his long legs were muscular too. The man had stayed in shape.

"Nope, I'm all by myself. Have a seat."

When the waiter arrived with Suzy's glass of chardonnay, Devon said, "Do you like rosé?" When Suzy nodded yes, he turned to the waiter and said, "Please put the chardonnay on my check, and we'll get two glasses of rosé from my vineyard."

"Of course, Mr. Gerrity. Great choice. I'll be right back."

When the wine arrived, Devon raised his glass to Suzy, toasting her, "Here's to old friends."

Suzy took a sip of the wine. "This is excellent, and I'm glad I ran into you, and not just for the wine," she laughed. "I've been meaning to apologize to you about my behavior the last time I saw you."

"Oh no. The apologies are all on my end. I know I seemed pushy and overbearing at a time when you were mourning your aunt. Forgive me."

"It wasn't that at all. When I said I could never sell you the land, what I meant was I can never sell it to anyone who wants it for a vineyard. Aunt Millie made that very clear in her will."

"That's a tough one. The real value of the land out here is converting these old potato farms to vineyards."

"I know. I honestly would have given the land to the park, which is what my aunt wanted me to do if I didn't keep it, but my son, Ian, loves it out here. He's going to stay for a while and renovate the farmhouse. He might even be joining Mitch Adams as a junior law partner."

"That's great news, Suzy. You're fortunate to have such a terrific kid, and I'm happy to show him the ropes out here. I know some good contractors too who won't rip him off."

"That would be great." Suzy took another sip of wine and

realized she had finished the glass.

"How about I order a bottle of rosé and we get something to eat? Claudio's has great lobster rolls and the wine goes perfect with them."

"Sounds good," said Suzy. *Damn, why am I not just going home?*

"So, tell me about the vineyard. How'd you get into that?"

"It was actually Carol's father. He had invested in a couple of the early vineyards out here, and then started buying up some of the potato farms. He was the one who encouraged us to start a vineyard. So, we spent time with some top vintners in Italy and France to learn the craft, and brought back some of their vines, and that was the start of Martinique's Vineyard. I had wanted to call it Gerrity's, but Carol said that sounded like an Irish pub."

"Is Carol still involved in the vineyard?"

"No. She's still a co-owner, but the truth is she never wanted to stay out here. She always thought it was too provincial, which was always a source of conflict for us. That and the fact that she never wanted to be tied down with children. When her father died five years ago, that's when she decided to end our marriage. She's now living in Paris. We should have ended it years before, but her father owned the majority and held it over our heads to keep us together. Now, tell me about your life."

By the time they had finished their lobster rolls and crab cakes, Suzy had told Devon about her wonderful marriage to Ken, the kids, her career, and The Three Tomatoes. He was a great listener, and so easy to talk to.

"I'm so impressed with all your successes, Suzy—your career, your marriage, your kids. But as I look at you right now,

I still have that image of the most gorgeous eighteen-year-old girl, standing on the edge of a dock in a bright red bathing suit, getting ready to dive into the bay. That was the summer I had finished college and realized how little Suzy had suddenly grown up."

"I remember that day too," said Suzy.

"I was such an ass that summer. I've thought about it so many times over the years. And I wish I had followed my heart instead of a path that had been carved out for me by others," he said as he looked at her with that tender look she still remembered only too well.

But she also remembered how he broke her heart, and the repercussions, and suddenly felt like she could barely breathe. She desperately wanted to change the subject. "That was a very long time ago, and we were just kids." And then she abruptly said, "I think I better get going."

"Let me just pay the check and I'll walk you to your car."

"No need for that. Thanks for dinner and the wonderful wine," she said as she hurried away.

CHAPTER 14
THE WINDS OF CHANGE

It was the middle of June, and Suzy had opened a bottle of wine and poured three glasses as she, Trish, and Madge settled on the terrace at the top of The Three Tomatoes loft. They had just finished their quarterly meeting as minority shareholders, along with Amy, plus North Star's CFO, and Jesse Middleton, who Suzy had come to think of as "the little weasel," although Madge's perception was much more colorful.

"That fucking little twit," was Madge's comment. They were all fuming.

They had reviewed subscriber growth, which was up 25 percent over the past quarter. They thought that was excellent, until Jesse got up with his PowerPoint presentation.

While he had acknowledged that the 25 percent growth in their core target of women over fifty was an excellent number, he proceeded to compare the potential growth rate with that of the younger thirtysomething young professional/young mother/working mom group.

"What's really significant is that it's this target group that advertisers want to reach. You have to admit, Suzy, there are a lot more advertisers for the upwardly mobile strivers than the menopause group."

"Yes, we are well aware of that, Jesse," Suzy had said as she tried to keep her outrage in check. "But it's those misconceptions we are trying to change with the media buyers. Our audience has disposable incomes, and they buy!"

The CFO had piped in, "While we like the growth in subscribers, and that's certainly a respectable number, the ad revenue side is slipping. How do you see that growing?"

Amy had taken over at that point, with their director of sales, and talked about the ad revenue growth opportunities they were pursuing.

Then the little weasel piped up to try to have the last word. "As our marketing team has discussed before, I think if you consider creating content for this younger demo, you'll see a huge jump in subscribers and revenues. Maybe more posts on how to be hot in the bedroom than how to handle hot flashes."

Madge couldn't help jumping in. "Here's a news flash for you, Jesse. Women over fifty don't need lessons on how to be hot in bed, we could give lessons."

Jesse had actually blushed at that.

"Once we start catering to a young demographic, we are no longer The Three Tomatoes," Suzy had said emphatically.

"Let's focus, then, on staying on track with continued subscriber growth and reaching your revenue projections," the CFO chimed in, trying to quell the tension in the room. "We'll see where we are going into the fourth quarter."

As they drank their wine on the terrace, they rehashed the meeting in detail.

"I don't get it," said Trish. "They acquired us because they said they wanted our valuable demographic, and now they want us to become something different? We've built this amazing brand that finally makes women over fifty no longer feel invisible or irrelevant, and now they're trying to marginalize us."

"Yes, and the worst part is that as minority shareholders, we might not have much say in the future of The Three Tomatoes," Madge sighed.

"Over my dead body," said Suzy. "We worked our butts off to create this brand and I'll be damned if I'm going to deal with another little snot-nosed weasel who doesn't get it."

They sipped their wine quietly for a few minutes.

"You know what we need?" said Madge, "We need a girls' getaway. We haven't done that in ages. The kids are just finishing the school term. Jason has a break from Washington, and I know he'd love some alone time with the kids, the campaign won't start gearing up 'til later in the summer, so I can definitely get away for two to three days. What about you two?"

"I'm in," said Suzy.

"Me too," chimed in Trish.

"And I know the perfect spot. There's a brand-new wellness hotel and spa in Montauk that's supposed to be fabulous. I'm sure I can get us in there," said Suzy.

Madge and Trish started laughing. "Hey, the last time you booked us into a spa, it was that spa from hell in Vermont with the forced marches up the mountain, and then we got kicked out for sneaking martinis into our room."

"I know I'll never live that one down...but, Madge, if it hadn't been for that trip, you might never have hooked up with Jason. This place has a full bar, and you don't need hiking boots...just flip-flops."

"Well, I guess that proves every disaster has its silver lining," Trish laughed.

With a phone call to the right person, Suzy scored the penthouse ocean view suite, with three bedrooms for the following weekend. It was good to have some clout through The Three Tomatoes. They had recently featured the hotel.

~~~~~~

Suzy had been spending longer days in the office. It was past 7:00 p.m. and she was still at her desk reviewing the advertising prospects. She might as well work, she thought, since she had no plans for the evenings now that she had told Bill she wasn't ready for a relationship. He had feigned a broken heart, with great drama, which they both ended up laughing about. He knew there wasn't much of a romantic relationship there, but they vowed to remain friends.

She was having trouble focusing on the numbers in front of her. She had not been able to stop thinking about Devon since their last encounter. Then almost as if she had conjured it, her cell phone rang with a number she didn't recognize, but it had a Long Island east end area code. She answered it and there he was.

"Suzy, I hope you don't mind, but I got your cell number from Ian. I know it's short notice, but I'll be in the city tomorrow for a meeting with one of our distributors. I was hoping you might be free for dinner tomorrow. There's a wonderful new restaurant that's just included our wines–it's called Trulia, and I have an 8:00 p.m. reservation. What do you say?"

Trulia was one of the hottest new restaurants in town and it was nearly impossible to get a reservation. But it wasn't the
~~~~~~

restaurant she wanted to see.

"Actually I am free. I've heard a lot of great things about the restaurant. Why don't you come to my apartment first and we can have a drink there? The restaurant is walking distance from my place. I'll text you the address."

"Perfect. I'll see you tomorrow night."

~~~~~~

Her heart was pounding, and she had changed outfits three times. She finally settled on a simple royal blue sheath that stopped just above her knees, which she paired with her black Louboutins, with their trademarked red soles, that showed off her long shapely legs. She was glad her hair had grown longer again. While she had liked the bob cut, it just hadn't felt like her. She had a long pendant that worked well with the dress and gave herself one last look in the mirror. *Well, this will have to do,* she thought just as the buzzer rang. "Yes, send him up," she said to the doorman.

He came bearing gifts. Actually, an entire case of his latest sparkling rosé, and he had chilled a bottle. He carried it into the kitchen, and opened the wine.

"Let's bring that out on the terrace," Suzy said, carrying fluted glasses.

They walked through the spacious living room out to the terrace.

"This is quite a view, you have."

"Yes, it was the big selling point for me when I bought the apartment earlier this year."

"Here's to the beautiful, accomplished woman you've become, Suzy." They clinked glasses.
~~~~~~

The conversation flowed and before they realized, it was time for their dinner reservation.

The restaurant more than lived up to its hype, but the electric vibes were all generated between Devon and Suzy. Their eyes sparkled as they talked. Devon told her how much he was enjoying getting to know Ian. They talked about the vineyards, and Suzy even shared some of the problems they were having with the acquisition.

"You know that's one of the reasons I've turned down offers to acquire us. I like being a boutique vineyard and calling the shots."

They lingered over their coffee until Suzy reluctantly said she thought she should head home. Devon had mentioned he was staying in a Midtown hotel in the other direction, but he insisted on walking her back to her building. He had his arm protectively around her waist and it sent shivers down her spine. It was still relatively early, and before she could censor herself, Suzy invited him up to the apartment for a nightcap.

They were barely inside the door when Devon embraced her and they were hungrily devouring each other, all the way to the bedroom.

Suzy stopped worrying whether she had remembered to shave her legs, if he'd notice her stretch marks after two children, and the little bit of fat she now carried around her middle. It certainly didn't seem to bother Devon who covered her entire body in kisses and caresses until she couldn't stand it a moment longer.

"Devon, I need you now," she whispered as he entered her. They were soon in unison with their rhythm, which brought them each to a climatic, fireworks ending.

They lay back, exhausted. "Suzy, you are amazing. And

you are far more beautiful now than you were at eighteen. Back then I thought you were the most beautiful girl I had ever laid eyes on and now you are the most beautiful woman."

She smiled. "I like that you've filled out your physique quite well, Mr. Gerrity, from that tall, slightly gangly young guy you were."

"You know," he said wistfully, "even after I married Carol, I always hoped I'd see you in the summers, but you never returned."

Suzy sat up and looked deeply into Devon's eyes. "You broke my heart that summer, and I couldn't bear the thought of seeing you with your wife. I would go out a couple of times during the year to see my aunt, but never in the summer."

Looking at Devon, she suddenly saw him as he looked that last summer night, when he told her he couldn't see her anymore because he was marrying Carol. She embarrassingly found herself tearing up.

"Oh, Suzy, I never meant for us to end that way," he said as he took her in his arms. "I should have been a lot more honest with you up front. I know it's more than thirty-five years late for an explanation, but I hope you'll hear me out."

Suzy dabbed her eyes and nodded.

"Carol's father, John Hopkins, was like a father to me. My dad was the town drunk, but John saw something in me and took me under his wing from the time I was a kid. He was the one who encouraged me to get good grades and apply for a scholarship at Brown, where he had gone. He even wrote a letter on my behalf. And then I worked for him every summer, which helped supplement my school bills. Carol was always there...we went to grammar school together and then dated through high school and college too. And when Carol's older brother died in a car crash, it just about broke John. But then he started to look to me as a son, and then it was just assumed that Carol and I would get married, and I'd join his business.

"That spring, after Carol and I graduated from college, I asked her to marry me. She laughed it off, and said she had a whole world to see that was way beyond this hick town and planned to spend the summer in Paris and then Italy in the fall. 'I've already told Daddy I'm not ready to settle down yet.'

"So, there I was, licking my wounds when suddenly you appeared that summer. I think I fell in love with you the moment I saw you dive off that dock in that little red bathing suit. It was the best summer of my life. And then two days after our magical moonlight evening on the beach, I got a letter from Carol, saying she was pregnant with our child and thinking of aborting it. I got the number of the hostel she was staying at and begged her to come home and marry me.

"I didn't want Carol to abort our baby. I had to do the right thing. Also there was her father, offering to take me into the business, and I admit my ambition factored into it too. We were married over Labor Day weekend and three days later she had a miscarriage. Then she told me she hadn't wanted to have that baby and never wanted to have children.

"I treated you terribly, Suzy. I was too much of a coward to be truthful. But I have to tell you there were so many times over the years when I couldn't help thinking, 'What if?' But then you wouldn't have met Ken and had the wonderful life you did with him."

By the time Devon finished, they both had tears in their eyes. "Devon, we've all made mistakes in our youth. You did do the right thing, in fact, the only thing you could have done." And she had done the only thing she could have done.

Devon took her in his arms. "I can't tell you how happy I am to have found you again."

By then it was dawn. They made passionate love again, and then Devon left to pick up his bag at the hotel room he hadn't slept in and headed back to Long Island.

They had agreed not to tell Ian yet, but Suzy promised she'd be out East for July Fourth, but this weekend was her girls' weekend getaway. She was already wondering how much to share with Madge and Trish.

CHAPTER 15
GIRLS' GETAWAY

Thanks to Madge, they had taken a private plane from Teterboro into Montauk Airport. Instead of the usual four-hour weekend drive, they arrived in forty minutes and were at the hotel before lunch. They still pinched themselves at the perks that came with Madge having married a billionaire, although it was never something Madge and Jason flaunted. They literally gave away thousands of dollars every year to the causes they supported. But as Madge said, *It's nice to treat ourselves once in a while.*

After an afternoon of massages, sauna, and the beach, they had enjoyed a lobster dinner at Navy Beach, one of Montauk's hot spots. As they walked through the restaurant, they could still turn heads. Trish was a petite size nothing, with that beautiful flaming red hair; Suzy's long highlighted blond hair flowed, and her long legs seemed to never end; and Madge, at five foot ten with raven hair had the presence of a queen. A couple of women who recognized them as The Three Tomatoes, interrupted their dinner to tell them they were big fans, something that still surprised them, but they never tired of hearing. Then the women added that they were supporting Jason's run for senator in November.

They returned to their beautiful suite and were sitting out on the terrace overlooking the Atlantic Ocean, enjoying a glass of wine. "Whoever would have thought during our days as roommates in our one-bedroom Hell's Kitchen walk-up when we were all starting out in the same ad agency and taking left-over food from conference meetings, that someday we'd be here?" said Trish.

"And let's not forget about all those awful house shares in the Hamptons too," added Suzy. They all laughed.

"This wellness hotel is wonderful," said Madge. "And it doesn't have all those draconian rules like that spa in Vermont."

"That was quite the experience," said Suzy, as they all laughed. "It's so great being here with the two of you."

Madge caught them up on all the campaign news. "Looks like it's certain that Frank Delano will run again Jason. It's bound to get ugly. He's known as a ruthless, dirty campaigner. And he's already trying to position Jason as an inexperienced idealist when it comes to getting things done in Washington, and that he 'stole' the idea that made him billions."

"That makes me see red. Jason is a such a good and decent human being, and a staunch supporter of women's rights," Trish piped in. "Plus he has a substantial track record in women's health care rights, something that Delano couldn't care less about. I think people will see right through those kind of smear tactics."

"Let's hope so," said Madge. "But I've seen some of the dirty tricks he's played and gotten away with. He likes to plant these totally unfounded rumors. But enough about me. Suzy, how is Ian doing with his new job and the renovations?"

"It's all going really well, except that he's beside himself because he's barely heard from Tatiana, and when he does, she seems very evasive."

"Interesting you should say that," said Trish. "She's been evasive with me too when I ask about her returning to New York in the fall. I'll try to call her next week and see if I can find out what's going on."

Suzy was looking at her phone and texting—something she had been doing all evening.

"Suzy, is everything all right?" asked Madge. "You've been uncharacteristically looking at your phone all night."

"Oh God, I'm sorry to be so rude. It's just..." and then she paused. *Well, if I can't tell my two best friends who can I tell?*

"It's just that there's a man who has come into my life. He's been texting me with sweet notes, but it's a bit complicated."

"What?" Trish and Madge said in unison.

"You just broke things off with Bill," said Trish. "How have you found time to find a new guy?"

"Actually, he's not a new guy, and it's a long story."

"We have all night," said Madge, as she poured more wine into their glasses.

~~~~~~

Their story started as kids. Devon was four years older than Suzy, but he was part of a group of locals and kids visiting for the summer who hung out at the beach every year. Devon always stood out as the ginger-haired kid with the zinc ointment on his nose to prevent sunburn, but he was always the leader
~~~~~~

of the group. As a twelve-year-old, she could remember hopping on her bike and following his lead as they all explored the winding roads of the North Fork. It was the days when kids were free to be kids and as long as you returned in time for dinner, no one worried.

And then there was that day when she was eighteen, the summer before her freshman year in college, when he finally noticed her. He had just graduated on a full scholarship from Brown, and was working that summer for Hopkins and Sons, the largest real estate developer on the east end of Long Island.

It started casually with long walks on the beach. And then meeting up on Saturdays for bike rides. That soon led to picnic lunches in secluded places and passionate make out sessions. Suzy would have gone further, but Devon always stopped. She thought it was because he didn't want to take advantage of her.

After one long Saturday afternoon, Suzy returned to the farmhouse, where her aunt was seated on the porch. "Come sit with me, Suzy. You know that boy is going to break your heart. His father is a no-good drunk, and that apple didn't fall far from the tree."

"Aunt Millie, how can you say that?"

"I don't mean with the drink, but whatever he's telling you, he's not being honest. He's a social climber, and everyone around here knows he'll marry that Carol Hopkins girl one of these days."

But Suzy didn't want to hear it. When she mentioned to Devon that she heard he had a girlfriend, he just said, "I only have one girl and she's standing right here."

Then in mid-August, a couple of weeks before she was

heading off to her freshman year in college, Devon suggested they have a moonlight dinner at the beach. He picked her up in his ten-year-old Jeep, which he drove right onto a secluded section of the beach. He laid out the blanket and pulled out a picnic basket with sandwiches and a bottle of wine. After a couple of glasses, it wasn't long before they were skinny-dipping. Then Devon carried her back to the blanket and told her he loved her. She threw her arms and her body around him and begged him to make love to her. He kept asking if she was sure, since he was fairly certain she was a virgin. *Yes, Devon, I love you too and I want you to be my first.*

"When he dropped me back home that night, I knew I wanted to be with him forever. A week went by and I didn't hear from him. I was beside myself, and then the following Saturday morning he showed up at my aunt's house and asked me to go for a ride. We drove down to the beach, and that's when he told me he was marrying Carol. I opened the car door. He tried to stop me from leaving, but I ran back to the house crying all the way. I spent the next three days in bed with Aunt Millie trying to console me and sending Devon away every time he came to the door.

"I had successfully avoided him all these years, rarely even visiting my aunt. But when I went back for the funeral, there he was. It was like time stood still. He and Carol are now divorced. We've had coffee and an accidental dinner in Greenport, but this past week we had dinner in New York. The sparks flew and I felt like that eighteen-year-old girl again. He spent the night at my apartment. That's when he told me the rest of the story."

Madge and Trish had sat there in astonishment as they listened to every word of Suzy's tale.

"I can't believe in all these years of telling each other everything, that you never told us about your first love," said Madge.

Suzy looked at her two best friends in the world, and finally said, "That's because there's more. And it's not a story I'm proud of.

"I finally pulled myself together and headed off to college. About six weeks into the semester, I started feeling nauseous and throwing up every morning. It was only when my roommate asked if I could possibly be pregnant that it hit me. That afternoon she went to Planned Parenthood with me, and the following day I had an abortion. I never told anyone else, not even Ken, until the weekend that Ian told us Emily was pregnant and they had decided to keep the baby. It brought back those dark days, and I broke down in tears after Ian had left. I told Ken about the abortion, but just said it had been a brief summer fling."

Even now, Suzy had a hard time telling her two best friends, who immediately hugged her.

"You did what was right at the time," said Madge.

"Yes, and I'm glad we had those options. I will always support a woman's right to choose, but it is something you live with forever. And now it's coming back to haunt me."

"What do you mean?" asked Trish.

"Devon told me he always wanted to have children, and it's his one regret in life. How can I tell him that he lost two children in the space of a few weeks?"

"If you really think you and Devon have a chance together, don't you think you both have to be honest after all these years?" Trish said gently.

Suzy sighed. "You're right, of course."

"When do we get to meet this guy?" said Madge.

"I want to take it slow for now. I'm not ready to tell Ian yet, although he and Devon have really bonded. Keri's another whole story. I just want to quietly enjoy getting to know him again. After all, it was Devon the boy I was in love with, and I was a young and naive girl he was in love with. We need to get to know who we've become during the past thirty-five-plus years."

"Well, we're happy for you," said Trish, "And we're always here for you.

CHAPTER 16

ANOTHER BROKEN HEART

It was the end of July when Ian got the text from Tatiana that broke his heart. She was not returning to New York in the fall. Her mother was ill. She had family obligations and promises to her mother that she had to keep. She said she would always hold Ian in her heart and cherish their time together, but they were from two very different cultures, and a future together was not possible.

Devon had stopped in to The Elbow Room for a late burger and beer, and spotted Ian there, alone at the bar downing tequila shots.

"Hey, buddy, don't you think you should slow it down a little?" he said as he pulled out the bar stool next to him.

That's when Ian spilled out the entire story to Devon.

"Listen, I know what it's like to have a broken heart, so I'm not going to give you any platitudes about it getting better and that plenty of other fish in the sea crap. But I am going to drive you home because you're in no shape to do that yourself."

After Devon got Ian safely home, he headed back to his own place. He was tempted to call Suzy and tell her, but he didn't want to break Ian's trust in him. He was going to need that trust when Suzy told Ian they were in a relationship. After sneaking around over the past month or so, they had agreed to go public with their newfound relationship.

~~~~~~

When Suzy arrived at The Three Tomatoes offices, she was excited to see that Trish was already there, working with their events planner.

"It's like old times," said Suzy.

Since the acquisition, Trish and Madge were rarely in the office, but with Harlem Week coming up in August, Trish wanted The Three Tomatoes to really promote it to their New York City subscribers, and she had created some special and unique experiences for Tomatoes who wanted to attend. "It's a great chance for our audience to experience the richness of Harlem—the food, the music, the art, and so much more."

It was around noon when Suzy got the text from Ian telling her that Tatiana had broken up with him and had no plans to return to New York.

Suzy made her way to the next level of the loft to find Trish. "Hey, think you can take a break for lunch?"

They headed around the corner to a local bistro and Suzy told Trish about Ian's text.

"What on earth? I knew something had to be going on, but for her to break up with Ian and give up on her dreams of an art career in New York is unthinkable. No wonder she's been avoiding me. I might just have to get on a plane to Montego Bay to find out what's going on."

Later that night, when Suzy phoned Devon as she climbed
~~~~~~

into bed, an every night ritual they had started when they were apart, she told him about Ian. He didn't tell her he had run into him or that Ian was drunk, and he had to drive him home.

"Devon, I know I said I would tell Ian about us this weekend, but I just don't think that this is the best time. I'm sure he's just devastated."

"It's a tough time for him, but if he finds out about us that will just add another layer of distrust he doesn't need right now."

"I guess you're right. I'll leave the city around noon on Thursday, so I'll have a longer weekend with him—and you too of course." But it wasn't just telling Ian about Devon that was on her mind. Suzy knew before she could do that, she had to tell Devon the rest of the secrets from their past.

~~~~~~

Trish had tried calling Tatiana and left a long message. Later that night she finally got a text from her saying she was sorry and appreciated everything Trish had done for her, but she had promises to keep to her mother.

Trish turned to Michael before she turned off the bedside lamp. "I need your advice."

Michael listened. "Well, you know I don't usually think it's a good idea to meddle in other people's lives, but it sounds like there's more to this than Tatiana is saying. So, if you really want to go to Montego Bay and try to talk to her, I'll support your decision. In fact, I'll go with you."

"Oh, Michael, that would be wonderful. I'll book us something right after the Harlem Festival in mid-August."
~~~~~~

Michael laughed, "And selfishly, I wouldn't mind playing eighteen holes of golf at Rose Hall either."

~~~~~~

Suzy got to the farmhouse in the late afternoon on Thursday. She had suggested to Ian that they meet in town for dinner after he finished work, since the old kitchen had been torn out. Ian was doing a remarkable job with the renovations. Maybe this, and his new job would help him get over Tatiana. At least she prayed it would.

When she arrived at the restaurant, Ian was already there. He stood up and gave her a big hug.

After their wine arrived, Suzy looked at her son. "Do you want to talk about it?"

"Not yet, Mom. It just hurts too much. Kind of like my head did the morning after I got drunk on tequila after I got her text. I have to thank Devon next time I see him for getting me home."

"What do you mean?"

"Oh, he ran into me at the bar at The Elbow Room and listened to me while I poured my heart out as I downed way too many tequila shots. And then he wisely insisted on driving me home that night, and even drove me back in the morning to pick up my car. He's a really good guy, Mom."

Suzy smiled to herself. *Yes he is indeed a good guy. Well, after I talk to Devon, maybe this conversation with Ian will go better than I thought.*

She and Ian stayed away from discussions about Tatiana and Devon and talked about the renovations and Ian's job at Mitch Adams's law office, which he was really enjoying.
~~~~~~

~~~~~~

The next night she met Devon at his beach cottage. He had ordered an amazing seafood dinner and had set up a table in the sand right in front of the cottage. He had bought it several years ago. It was one of the old, dilapidated cottages that have dotted these parts since the 1940s. He had kept the character, but had modernized it, raising the ceilings, and putting in picture windows and sliding glass doors to take full advantage of the water views.

After they had finished dinner, Devon suggested they take a stroll on the beach. It was the same beach they had played on as children, and the same beach they had fallen in love on. They strolled hand in hand for a while, and then sat down to watch the sunset. *Well, I can't put this off any longer.*

"Devon, I don't want there to be any dark corners lingering from our past. "

"Suzy, I've told you everything."

"I know, but I haven't told you everything."

With great trepidation, she told him the rest of the story. When she finished, he just sat there in silence. And then she saw the tears streaming down his face.

"I was such a fool, Suzy. To think that I could have had you and our child, and I blew it. I blew it with Carol too, marrying her when I knew I loved you."

Suzy put her arms around him. "I just hope you can forgive me for what I did."

"Oh, Suzy, if you had only called me then...I would have been there. But we can't go back and change the past. I'm just glad we're here now."
~~~~~~

They embraced, and as the sun went down, they made love in the sand, like they had done so many, many years before.

~~~~~~

The next day she told Ian she was seeing Devon, and then told him about their history together, including her abortion.

Ian looked stunned.

"You know, Ian, it was much different back then when a girl got pregnant. And while it wasn't easy for you and Emily to decide to have a child together and not get married, it wasn't like that in my day. It was a stigma and the end of many girls' dreams. Making that decision allowed me to finish college, and then meet your father who I loved with all of my heart, and then to have you and Keri when I was ready."

"Mom, I'm not judging you. It's just a lot to absorb at one time. You deserve to be happy. To be honest, I thought that guy Bill you were dating for a while was a pompous ass, but I like Devon a lot."

"I'm glad to hear that. He likes you too. I know you don't want to talk about Tatiana yet, but I do understand what it's like to have a broken heart."

"Thanks, Mom. And thanks for being honest with me about your past."

"Let's hope Keri will feel that way too," Suzy said with a sigh.
~~~~~~

CHAPTER 17
TURMOIL

Summer had disappeared in a whirlwind of frenetic activity. But now that September was here, summer seemed like the calm before the storm. Madge had been making appearances all over the state on behalf of Jason. The more time Suzy and Devon spent together, the more they realized how much they loved the people they had become. Trish had just returned from seeing Tatiana in Montego Bay. They were all looking forward to their first Ripe Tomatoes dinner since the spring, and to their traditional martini meetup before dinner.

Suzy suggested they meet at her apartment for the martinis to avoid any media frenzy around Madge, so they could catch up in private.

They sat out on the terrace and Trish and Madge both commented that Suzy looked positively glowing. "It's great to see you looking happy again," Trish said as they clinked glasses.

"It's great to feel happy—something I never thought I'd feel again after Ken died. Now tell us what happened in Jamaica."

"It doesn't have the ending I had hoped for," said Trish as she unfolded the events.

Tatiana was totally surprised when she got the call from Trish telling her she was in Montego Bay and inviting her to lunch the next day. Trish had suggested they have lunch sent up to her hotel suite, so they'd have privacy.

As soon as Trish greeted her with a huge hug, Tatiana collapsed in a pool of tears, and Trish slowly coaxed the story out of her.

Her brothers had asked her to come home for a while because their mother was having heart issues, and she had also somehow gotten wind of her relationship with Ian. She wasted little time telling her that no daughter of hers was going to be used up by some rich white boy in New York City, who would just cast her aside, the same way her aunt Tania had been cast aside shortly after she arrived in that sinful city.

Tatiana was shocked by her mother's harsh words, and especially about her own sister, who she said had lived a wild bohemian artist's life in New York sleeping with any man she wanted to, and never getting married or having a family. She was not letting that happen to her only daughter.

She then informed her that Nigel Duncan was back on the island and had been asking about her.

Nigel Duncan was heir to the largest rum estate in Jamaica. They were one of the oldest and most successful families on the island. Her mother had worked on the estate as a cook for many years. She used to bring Tatiana with her as a young child, and later she would go there after school to do her studies. She and Nigel had been playmates since the age of four. He was sent to boarding school in England when he got older, and she would only occasionally see him on school breaks.

Then one day when she was in her last year at the Royal College of Art in London, she was invited to a gallery opening in Soho where she ran into Nigel, who was now attending Oxford. They were so excited to see each other and to see someone from home, that they made a date for the following weekend. Soon they were seeing each other almost every weekend.

When they both went home for Christmas break and Nigel appeared on her doorstep to take her to dinner one evening, her mother was ecstatic! "That boy is moonstruck over you," she said as she danced around the kitchen the next morning preparing breakfast. "He can give you the kind of life you deserve."

And Nigel was "moonstruck." But as much as Tatiana enjoyed his company, she saw him more as a brother than a potential husband. Her dream was to get a scholarship to Parsons and enter the art scene in New York City, just like her aunt.

She told Nigel about her big dreams, and when she got her scholarship, he was happy for her and even a little envious. The night she got the news he took her to dinner in London to celebrate. "My path has already been laid out for me. I will return home after school and start training to take over the family business. But when you return home one day, I will be there, waiting for you," he had said.

A couple of days after her arrival from New York, she got a text from Nigel asking if they could meet at one of the local jerk chicken spots that were popular at the beaches. They hugged warmly, and then Nigel told her his family had heard about her mother's health issues. They didn't really trust the local doctors and they wanted to send her to a specialist in London, at their expense. "After all, your mother has been part of our family for many years."

Nigel went back to the house with her. It took quite a while for her mother to accept his offer—but only if Nigel and Tatiana agreed to go with her.

The doctors said she needed a heart valve replacement. It was serious surgery and made more complicated because her mother was overweight and a diabetic.

The night before the surgery, Tatiana's mother made her promise that if she made it through, she'd stay on the island, and maybe even think about marrying Nigel. Her mother was in such a state that Tatiana agreed to the staying on the island part, but added she and Nigel had never discussed marriage.

Her mother pulled through fine, and when she was well enough to travel, Nigel arranged for a private plane to fly her home. Every day he would visit to check on her progress, and of course the chance to be near Tatiana.

A month later he invited her to dinner and proposed. "I love you, Tatiana. I know you don't feel the same way about me as I do for you, but I promise to be a good husband, and I will always take care of you and your family. I think in time you will grow to love me as I love you."

"An agonizing week later, she said yes, and now they are planning a New Year's wedding," Trish said sadly as she concluded the story.

Suzy shook her head. "I can't believe she's throwing away her dreams like that. Who knows if she and Ian would have had a future together, but she certainly has a wonderful future as an artist."

"Believe me," said Trish. "I talked to her about that until I was blue in the face. She has this misguided notion that she owes this to her mother."

"I guess I'm going to have to tell Ian. I think he was still hopeful she'd return, but he can't sit around waiting for her."

"Actually, Tatiana gave me a letter addressed to Ian. Even the envelope is tearstained," Trish said as she handed it to Suzy. "Or would you rather I give Ian the letter?"

Suzy sighed. "No, I'll give it to him this weekend. And to make this week even more fun, we have our quarterly P&L meeting with North Star," said Suzy. "And I don't have a good feeling about it.

"Let's not think of any of that tonight," said Madge, "and just enjoy dinner and seeing what the Ripe Tomatoes are up to."

~~~~~~

They were back at their usual Midtown haunt, seated at their usual round table in the center of the restaurant, which Hope always chose so she could see and be seen! Their waiter knew what drink each of them preferred and brought them to the table almost as soon as they were seated. This evening's group included Hope, Celeste (who had just returned to New York after spending the summer in London), Arlene, and Heather Stone. They were all happy she was able to join them tonight, now that she was spending so much time in Washington as a bureau chief.

Just before they sat down, Heather said quietly to Madge, "Can you join me for a private drink after dinner?"

Madge nodded yes. *I wonder what that's about?*

After cheers and clinking of glasses, they all wanted to know how Hope's show was going. "Frankly," said Celeste, "I'm surprised that you and Ellen haven't killed each other yet."
~~~~~~

"Oh, believe me, I've dreamed up all kinds of 'accidental' deaths for her, since that first leak to the press about my wanting to get rid of our director. Thank God I was able to sweet-talk him back. Ellen swears it wasn't her. But just about every week there's some kind of leak to the press that always puts me in a bad light. The latest is that I'm not happy with our star, and nothing could be further from the truth. We don't need that kind of demoralizing press, especially with previews starting in a couple of weeks."

"But why would she want to leak negative things about the show?" said Arlene. "She has as much of a stake in its success as you do."

"When you put it rationally, yes. But she works on emotions and she's always been jealous of me," said Hope, heading for a rant.

Trish knew it was time to change topics. "Celeste, tell us about your summer in London."

"The town is all abuzz about the latest escapades of Meghan and Harry. Of course, they continue to blame Meghan, as if she's leading him around by the nose."

That led to a lively conversation about how the Brits hate it when an American "snags" a royal, plus the whole sexism aspect of turning Meghan into an evil bitch who has Harry in her control.

"Whenever I dare to say perhaps it's Harry who wants to live his own life, they all give me those condescending looks that the English are so good at," said Celeste. "But I do love to stir up the pot, and Oliver delights in it."

"That is why we adore you, Celeste," said Hope.

"And, Arlene, how was your summer?"

"It was absolutely wonderful. I spent most of it sailing

with Bill Stanton."

Everyone except Trish and Madge suddenly looked at Suzy and then Arlene with surprise.

"Wait," said Heather, "wasn't it Suzy who was dating Bill?"

Suzy and Arlene both laughed.

"Well, I did have a brief thing with him," said Suzy, "but then we decided we'd rather just be old friends. He has a summer home very near Arlene's and they both love to sail, so I sorta set them up."

"I'm so glad she did," said Arlene. "He's a charming man, and now I can get off those horrible online dating sites."

Everyone was delighted.

Then it was Suzy's turn. She updated them on the renovations at the farmhouse, and how Ian was enjoying the law firm. She wasn't ready to tell them about Devon, especially Hope who would have a million questions.

They continued to share news and gossip over dinner, along with a lot of laughter. After they all said their goodnights, Heather and Madge lingered behind.

"Let's have a drink at the bar," Heather said.

They each ordered a nightcap.

"Okay, what's up?" said Madge.

"This could just be a rumor, but I heard some scuttlebutt that one of the tabloids is about to do a front-page story that you and Jason bought your kids from that orphanage in Ethiopia and that Yonas's mother is alive."

Madge felt her face draining of blood. "That's ridiculous. God, even Frank Delano wouldn't stoop that low."

"Listen," said Heather, "who knows if they even have enough to run with this story, but I didn't want you and Jason to be blindsided."

CHAPTER 18

YOU'RE FIRED!

Suzy and Amy made their way up in the elevator to one of the conference room floors of North Star Entertainment. Neither had said much and they were both feeling glum about the meeting ahead.

They walked into the conference room and were greeted by Jesse and his team of minions, along with North Star's CFO, who was already pouring over Excel spreadsheets.

Suzy suddenly had an image in her head of Jesse with devil's horns, and Mr. CFO in a green eye shade. She almost laughed at loud, but it helped her rebuild her confidence for what she knew was about to be a contentious meeting. It did not disappoint.

"The bottom line is the subscriber numbers are flat, and advertising revenues are down. So, it's time to make some changes in the marketing direction of The Three Tomatoes," said Jesse sounding almost gleeful.

He and his minions then presented yet another tedious PowerPoint presentation with their plan for a repositioning of the brand to the hip and trendy thirtysomething woman.

That repositioning would start with significant changes to The Three Tomatoes content.

"We're moving over one of our top content managers from our women's entertainment division to head up the content team. We're also recruiting for a new head of advertising sales, and we're looking for someone with a lot of experience in the millennial demographic."

Suzy and Amy sat there stunned. "Well, that makes no sense since the reason North Star acquired us was to have access to our loyal audience of women over forty-five, and content aimed at millennials will turn them away."

"Yes, we know that, but now that we've converted a high percentage of those women to our streaming media services, we've also used their profiles to create a series of models to market directly to women with similar profiles. It's a much more efficient model to reach that target audience than by continuing the struggle for new older subscribers to The Three Tomatoes and an uphill battle for advertisers."

Just as Jessie finished his sanctimonious and condescending lecture, Suzy realized that Matt Greene, North Star's CEO, had entered the room.

He greeted Suzy and Amy warmly. Jesse and his minions and the green-visored CFO had barely left the room when Suzy, as calmly as she could, turned to Matt.

"I don't understand, Matt. A few months ago, you were wooing us and singing the importance of older women in your marketing plans, and now you do a one-eighty? What changed your tune?"

"Listen, it wasn't a decision we made lightly. But you've seen the numbers. We still love The Three Tomatoes brand, and we think of this new direction as a brand extension that will make us relevant to a younger demographic. As Jesse showed, with the sophistication of data mining software, we can reach the older woman demographic in a more economical way. And as minority shareholders, this move should ultimately increase the value of your shares over time."

Amy started to protest, but Matt put his hand up.

"There's more. I didn't expect either of you to be in agreement with this shift in strategy, or to support it. So, we are prepared to offer you a healthy exit package to buy out your contracts. My assistant will give you the packages before you leave. I hope you both agree it is in the best interest of everyone," and with that he got up and left the room.

Suzy and Amy made their way downstairs and around the corner to a local Starbucks. They had barely sat down when Amy started crying angry tears. "We've been betrayed."

"Well, we've certainly had the rug pulled out. Listen, head home for now, Amy. I'll call Trish and Madge for an emergency meeting, hopefully at my place this evening."

~~~~~~

Suzy texted Madge and Trish with the words, "We've been screwed over by North Star. Emergency meeting tonight at seven, my apartment. Can you be there?"

Madge had just left a senior center in Brooklyn, where she had talked to residents about why they should vote for Jason, when she got Suzy's text. She responded yes immediately. *Oh God, I don't need more stress this week.*

She had been a bundle of nerves since her conversation with Heather earlier in the week, even though Jason had remained calm and reassuring after she told him what Heather
~~~~~~

had said.

"Listen, hon, this is tabloid sensationalism and maybe even dirty politics at its worst. We went through all the right channels to adopt Yonas and Bitania. If they print this unfounded story, we'll fight it," he had said taking her into his arms.

But Jason's attempt at reassurance hadn't calmed Madge. Every morning this week she had checked the tabloids, held her breath, and then breathed when there was no mention of the story. But she couldn't help worrying. W*hat if Yonas's mother is actually alive*?

~~~~~~

Suzy poured wine all around, and then she and Amy gave the blow-by-blow account of what had transpired.

"Those fucking assholes," said Madge when they finished.

"They're going to destroy everything we worked so hard to build," added Trish. "How do we stop this?"

"I honestly don't know if we have any recourse. It's like watching a train wreck. We're going to have to meet with our lawyers, but as minority shareholders we gave up our rights on what they want to do with the company. Amy and I have to meet with them anyway to review the packages they offered us. Which are quite generous by the way, but I feel like they're buying our silence—it comes with all kinds of confidentiality agreements."

"Fuck them," said Amy. "I want to shout to the world that North Star Entertainment doesn't give a rat's ass about older women."

"There's not much we can do until you talk to the lawyers,"
~~~~~~

said Trish, always the calming one in the group. "We all need to take a few cleansing breaths and clear our minds so we can find the right path out of this. And Madge, on a plus note, North Star now has your documentary, *The Lost Generation,* in its streaming lineup so a lot more people will see it."

Madge suddenly turned away.

"Honey, what is it?" Suzy said gently when she realized Madge was sobbing.

Madge's award-winning documentary was all about the children of Ethiopia and other war-torn countries who were left as orphans, many of them living on the streets to fend for themselves. The lucky ones found their way into substandard orphanages while others became victims of sex traffickers. It was during that filming that she had visited the orphanage where Yonas had captured her heart. It was the same orphanage they had returned to two years later and adopted Bitania.

The mention of the documentary brought everything back to the surface, and Madge told them about the possible tabloid story.

They rallied around her with assurances that the story would most likely never run, and it was just tabloid fodder.

They were all trying to be positive when they said their good-nights, but it was a half-hearted attempt.

The only good part of the day was when Suzy talked to Devon later that night and caught him up on her miserable day. "And on top of that, I have to give Ian the letter from Tatiana this weekend."

"I'll be here for you, and for Ian too. And I have a few ideas on how to make you feel a little better this weekend," he said in that sexy low voice of his.

CHAPTER 19

EVERYTHING HITS THE FAN

When Madge's phone started blowing up at 5:00 a.m. she knew it was the news she was dreading. And there it was on the front page of the country's biggest sleaze tabloid—Senator Madison Bought His Kids in Ethiopia: Heartbroken Mom Wants Her Son Back. It was accompanied by a crying woman clutching a photo of Yonas.

She immediately called Jason in Washington.

"I know, my phone started blowing up too this morning. As soon as we're out of session today I'll head home. I've already put private investigators on the case and my press people are putting out a statement to the effect that the story is unfounded."

"But, Jason, what if Yonas's mother is alive?"

"Let's just take this one step at a time. We should know more by this evening, and then we can put a plan of action together. "

Madge's head was spinning. It was one thing to have Jason's campaign derailed because of this, but to possibly lose their child? That was unthinkable.

One of the people who had texted her earlier about the story was Heather Stone. She was the next person on Madge's list to call.

"This is what I was afraid of, Madge. But listen, you and I both know investigative journalists who work in that part of the world. Let's put our contacts together because if anyone can get to the truth of this story it will be one of them."

Within an hour she and Heather were working their lists. *At least it's a start.*

And then she texted her two best friends.

~~~~~~

Trish dropped everything and headed to Brooklyn to console her friend.

Suzy was already on her way to the North Fork, but immediately called Madge.

"Listen, I can turn around right now and be there in less than an hour," Suzy said after she heard the story.

"I know you would, but there's no need to do that. I just wanted you to hear this from me. And you have to deliver Tatiana's letter to Ian and deal with that aftermath this weekend. I'll be fine, really. Trish will be here shortly, and Heather and I are trying to get to some people on the ground there to get the real story. Jason will be home tonight."

"All right," Suzy said reluctantly, "but call me anytime and if you get any updates let me know."

Madge felt her first little bit of calm all morning knowing that she and Trish and Suzy had always been there for each other and always would.
~~~~~~

~~~~~~

Suzy arrived just in time to have lunch with Devon at the vineyard. He had set up a table out among the vines and had one of his best sauvignon blancs ready to pour. Over salads she told him about the tabloid story and how Jason and Madge had adopted their children.

"Devon, it's so unfair the way Jason and Madge are being vilified as child stealers. It's atrocious what happens in places like Ethiopia where children are left with no family because of HIV-AIDS, wars, and famines. No one has done more than Madge and Jason to shine a light into the dark recesses to try to help these kids. Yonas and Bitania were the lucky ones because they ended up in an orphanage instead of on the streets or worse, and then of course were even luckier to be adopted by loving parents.

"Madge and Jason were on a fact-finding mission with the UN when they visited the orphanage that Yonas was in and he stole their hearts. They did everything through all the right channels when they adopted him and then later Bitania. And they have donated hundreds of thousands of dollars to upgrade several of the orphanages in that area that have very few resources," she sighed dejectedly as she finished.

"You have definitely had a hell of a week," Devon said as he gently took her hand, "and now you have to tell Ian the girl he loves is marrying someone else. How can I help you through all of this?"

"You already are, just by being here and listening to me."

"Well, I'm happy to do more than listen," he said and leaned in with that mischievous glint in his eyes that she loved, and kissed her.
~~~~~~

~~~~~~

When Suzy handed the letter to Ian, he said he was going to the beach to read it.

When two hours passed and he hadn't returned, Suzy was about to go looking for him when he came through the front door.

"Mom, before you say anything, I don't want to talk about this. Not now, not later, not ever. I'll be okay, but I need some time alone."

"I understand. I'll go to Devon's for the night and give you some space. And if you're up to it tomorrow, let's go for a long bike ride. It's supposed to be a beautiful fall day."

"Okay, Mom. Thanks for understanding," he said and headed to his room.

She just wanted to hug him and kiss the "boo-boo" to make it all better just like when he was little. *It doesn't matter how old your kids are, when they hurt, you hurt.*

~~~~~~

When Suzy returned to the farmhouse the next morning, she was pleasantly surprised to see Ian up and about.

"You're right, Mom, it's a great day for a bike ride. If you're still up to it, I'll get the bikes and meet you out front."

Suzy went to the guest room to change and let out a huge sigh of relief.

They stopped to get sandwiches for lunch and two hours later, they were sitting on the nearly deserted beach at Orient Beach State Park, where you can see four lighthouses in one of the most beautiful natural wonderlands anywhere.

They sat quietly for a while, just soaking in the nature around them.

"So, Mom, I have a business proposition I want to talk to you about."

Suzy was so relieved that Ian wanted to talk about something other than his broken heart, she would have entertained any business proposition, but this one was a complete surprise.

"I really love it out here, and I keep thinking how we can make all that land around the farmhouse into something sustainable and eventually profitable, without violating Aunt Millie's wishes about not selling the land to any of the vineyards. But it's a catch-22 because it's the vineyards that make the land valuable. So, I've been thinking, what if we start our own vineyard on the land?"

Ian went on to explain that he and Mitch Adams had carefully reviewed Aunt Millie's will and legal precedents and saw nothing legally that would prevent them from starting a vineyard or morally violating Aunt Millie's wishes. He had also been spending hours with Devon to learn more about the wine business, the economics, and what would be involved.

"Mom, I've put together a business plan that I'd like to go over with you. We can have Devon there too so you can ask questions about this from his perspective as a successful vintner."

Suzy was stunned. And amazed. And proud too.

When she didn't say anything, Ian said, "Listen, Mom, the farmhouse and the land belong to you. And if you think this is a terrible idea, I understand. Really I do."

"Oh, Ian, I just needed to catch my breath first. Actually, I think it might be a really great idea. Let's get back to the house and take a look at that business plan."

~~~~~~

Later that afternoon, Suzy, Ian, and Devon sat at the dining room table in the farmhouse as Ian took Suzy through the business plan. It was very thorough, and Suzy suspected there had been a lot of input from Devon, but she had to admit she was impressed. She asked a lot of questions, most of which Ian could answer, and only occasionally deferred to Devon for his thoughts based on his experience.

Suzy's first concern had been the start-up costs, especially with The Three Tomatoes debacle, but she was pleased to see that the plans started with just a few acres at a time, and a lot of the costs would be covered by the acres that were still being leased by local farmers. Devon had even offered to provide mature vines from his vineyard to hasten the first vintage.

Just as the sun was starting to set, Suzy sat back and said, "Well, Ian, it looks like we're going to be in the wine business. Or I should say, you are going to be in the wine business. I think we need to go out and celebrate with a huge lobster dinner and the best wines from the North Fork."

Devon went home to change and volunteered to pick them up for dinner. Suzy was sitting quietly on the porch waiting for Ian to finish dressing and for Devon to arrive, when a cardinal landed on the back of the rocker next to her, intently peering at her before it flew off. *That's the second time a cardinal has suddenly appeared in front of me. I wonder what that means?*

Later that night, wrapped in Devon's arms after having
~~~~~~

made passionate love, she said, “I can’t tell you how much it means to me that you have taken Ian under your wing. I love seeing the relationship that’s developed between the two of you.”

“It’s been all my pleasure. If I had a son, I couldn’t image a better one than Ian. You and Ken raised a terrific young man.”

Suzy choked up with emotion and tried not to let her tears fall on Devon’s chest.

~~~~~~

When Jason arrived home Friday night, he dropped his bag at the front door and he and Madge held each other for what seemed like the longest time, until Yonas came bounding down the steps.

“Hey, Dad, can we go to the batting range tomorrow, please, please, please?”

Right behind him was Bitania, followed closely by the dog, all wanting attention.

“Hey kids, let’s give Dad a little break first. He just walked in the door. We can talk about baseball and everything else over dinner,” said Madge.

Just then Bertha appeared and told the kids they could come help her make cookies for dessert and they all followed her into the kitchen.

“Why don’t you change, and then meet me in the den. The story is trending now and it’s all over the mainstream media.”

A few minutes later, Jason and Madge were ensconced on the comfy couch in the den to catch up on what they had each learned so far.

“So, we know that ever since Ethiopia decided to ban for-
~~~~~~

eign adoptions, they've come under a lot of humanitarian pressure to change their policies," said Jason.

"And rightly so," Madge piped in. "Most of those children will remain in orphanages because their culture doesn't generally believe in adopting."

"Well, apparently there's a faction in Ethiopia's parliament that feels they are being unfairly attacked by these groups, and they are trying to get negative stories out there about high-profile foreigners who have adopted Ethiopian children. So, by targeting us and feeding this story to a tabloid, they are assured it would be splashed all over their pages and then get picked up by the mainstream press here and internationally too.

"It's definitely politically motivated, but we are just not sure if it's dirty politics here, or dirty politics there, or maybe a little of both. They're trying to track down the alleged mother too. Hopefully we'll get to the bottom of this soon. In the meantime though, we need to deal with the media. I told my press team we'll meet with them tomorrow and prepare a press conference for Monday morning."

Madge agreed the smart thing to do was for the two of them to try to get in front of this story.

"Heather and I are working our contacts with some reporters on the ground there to find out who this woman is who claims to be Yonas's mother. And I contacted the new director of the orphanage to see if there are any more records about Yonas's background. She said it's doubtful, but she would check.

"And we're going to have to talk to Yonas before he hears something from a friend or something on the news. That's the most difficult part."

Jason took her in his arms. "I know, but we're a family and we'll get through this."

Then they strategized on what to say to Yonas and agreed they would talk to him together before bedtime.

Dinner was a lively chatterfest with both kids competing for Jason's attention to tell him all about their week. The dog had his head in Jason's lap for his share of attention too not to mention that Jason was sneaking tidbits to him from his plate. Madge couldn't help but smile watching her beautiful family. Just as they were finishing dinner, Madge's phone pinged. Normally she wouldn't have it at the dinner table, but with everything that was going on she had made an exception. It was Heather. "Call me," the text read.

"I'm just going to make a call. Think you can handle these two little monsters?" she said as she stepped back into the den to call Heather.

"Sorry to bother you at dinnertime," said Heather, "but I've been thinking. What we need are the two best investigative reporters we know to find out what's behind this story."

"I agree, Heather, and we've both briefed a couple of reporters we know who are in the region and willing to help."

"Okay, you're not getting it, Madge. You and I are the two best people to get to the bottom of this story. I've already told my boss I need a few days off to pursue this. You and I need to head to Ethiopia."

CHAPTER 20

IN SEARCH OF THE TRUTH

Suzy and Amy weren't surprised by the news delivered to them by one of the top contract attorneys from Ken's former law firm.

"I'm sorry to say this, Suzy, but when you agreed to sell the majority interest in The Three Tomatoes to North Star, you gave up control of the business. They have the final word on what direction they want to take it in. And as to the generous contract buyouts, I say take them."

"But that means not only can't we say anything disparaging about those scoundrels, we also can't start a competitive business or go to work for a competitor for two years," Suzy said with distaste.

"Listen, you all have shares in the company and you don't want to see those tank because of bad press. With the buyout packages, and the potential to make a lot of money with your shares, that opens doors to do whatever you want. I know it's not the answer either of you wanted to hear, but it's the best advice I can give."

They both thanked him for his straightforward advice and

headed to the elevators.

"You know what we need?" Suzy said to Amy.

"A good stiff drink?"

"Well, that and shoes. Nothing cheers me up more than Manolos and Louboutins."

And with that they headed to Bergdorf.

In the middle of trying on shoes, they had decided to the take the buyouts.

With their new shoe purchases tucked into Bergdorf shopping bags, they were seated at Bergdorf's elegant restaurant on the seventh floor overlooking Central Park.

"This calls for Bellinis," said Suzy, and they clinked glasses when they arrived.

"You know, Suzy, you really changed my life in the best way possible. You saw something in me at that horrid little ad agency we worked in and brought me into The Three Tomatoes and helped me grow in ways I could never have imagined. I'll miss it, and I have no idea what I'll do next, but the money will give me the freedom to think about it without having to worry about how to pay the rent."

"Well, here's to freedom," said Suzy. "And by the way, Jason still owns the loft, so once they move The Three Tomatoes staff out, if any of them are left after this, we can still use that as office space for whatever we dream up next."

"I'll toast to that," said Amy.

~~~~~~

The reporters and cameras were everywhere, and despite some reporters shouting questions like, "How much did you pay for your kids?" and "Are you giving your son back to his
~~~~~~

mother?" Jason and Madge managed to stay calm and not punch anyone out during the press conference.

"I'm so glad I'm not part of the fucking asshole media crowd anymore," said Madge once they were alone in the car and heading to the airport where she would meet Heather and board Jason's private jet to Ethiopia.

"It wasn't easy to stay cool, but it would have given them more fodder to sell newspapers," said Jason. "Madge, are you sure this is the right thing to do?"

"Jason, I have to find out the real story and meet this woman who may or may not be our son's mother. But either way, we have to know. I hate leaving the kids right now, especially since you'll be back in Washington, but I'm grateful your parents offered to stay with them while I'm gone."

Jason walked into the private waiting area with Madge. Heather was already there, along with a couple of security guys Jason had insisted on hiring. "Thanks for doing this, Heather. And both of you stay safe."

Madge waited to board last, and when Jason took her in his arms, she almost lost it. Regaining her composure, she promised to stay safe and find the truth.

~~~~~~

"It sure didn't take long for North Star to get their press release out," Suzy said to Trish with disdain as she unfolded the article in *The Wall Street Journal* with the headline Cofounder Exits The Three Tomatoes After North Star Acquisition. Suzy read some of the highlights as they drank coffee in Trish's gallery office.

"The quotes just make me want to barf. 'We're so grateful
~~~~~~

for Suzy Hamilton's guidance over the past three months as we transitioned The Three Tomatoes into the North Star family,' blah, blah, blah. But the one that really makes me sick is the one attributed to me. 'I know The Three Tomatoes will rise to new levels of excellence as younger audiences discover this cheeky, irreverent brand.' And then they announced the new CEO who is replacing Amy—and it's that little weasel Jesse. Just unbelievable!"

Trish just shook her head in disbelief. "It makes me so sad to think about how we started this little brand and then grew it just to see it get screwed up by corporate sharks. I wish we had never let it go."

"I know. But if we look at the bright side, the sale is what made it possible for you to open this beautiful gallery, and I know the art world is your first love."

"Yes, and I do love it," said Trish. "So, now that you're a woman of leisure, what do you think you'll do?"

"It's such a strange feeling. I've worked since I was sixteen years old, and this is the first time I haven't had a job or an office to go to. But it will give me more time to spend with Devon, and time to help Ian with starting up the vineyard too. Not to mention that Keri and Chris are coming out to the farmhouse this weekend—Keri hasn't been there since Aunt Millie left it to me. And they want to talk about their wedding plans for the spring—they want something small and intimate, and I was thinking Devon's vineyard would be a perfect setting."

"That's so exciting," said Trish. "Have you told her about Devon yet?"

"No, but I will this weekend. It wasn't something I wanted to tell her over the phone. And I wanted her to meet Devon too."

"I hope that goes well. And now please tell me how it went with Ian after you gave him Tatiana's letter."

Suzy gave her the details. "I know he has a broken heart that he's trying to hide, but I think his job with Mitch's law firm and starting the vineyard will keep him very busy and hopefully take his mind off this."

Trish sighed. "I still can't believe Tatiana is giving up her dreams because of her manipulative mother. I just sold two more of her paintings this week. It's such a pity."

Suzy nodded in agreement. "And I do wish we'd hear something about Madge's Ethiopia trip. Let's hope this is all a hoax."

"Jason has promised to update us the second he hears anything."

CHAPTER 21
ETHIOPIA

It had been nearly four years since Madge had been to the orphanage where they found Yonas and then Bitania. They had seen a lot of the photographs of the changes that had been made thanks largely to their donations, but seeing it in person was an entirely different experience starting with the moment they pulled up to the front of the building. Instead of the desolate dirt and dusty area that once greeted visitors, they now had a pathway lined with stones and the once drab cinder block building had been painted white with a cheery blue trim.

The new director was delighted to meet Madge in person, and proudly gave them a tour. A beautiful new wing had been added to the building and greatly alleviated the overcrowded conditions that had existed when Yonas was there. Dormitory-style rooms and bunk beds for the older children had replaced wide open rooms with mats on the floor and children of all ages everywhere. Now there was a separate area for babies and toddlers with cribs. More staff had been added so that babies could be held and cuddled instead of being left alone to cry for hours.

"We have real classrooms too for the children, and books for them to read," said the director as she continued the tour and led them into the play yard.

Madge marveled at the children on swings and sliding boards, and the boys playing soccer with real soccer balls in a field nearby. "It's wonderful to see all these enhancements," she said as they made their way back to the director's office.

"I wish I had better news for you, Mrs. Madison, but our records of Yonas are slim at best. He was found by a UN humanitarian team in a small village not far from here. He and several other severely malnourished children were living in a hut where village women took turns caring for them as best they could. But food was scarce, and they had their own children to feed. Yonas was sent to a hospital to recover and eventually brought here."

"We were told that his father had died in the war," said Madge, "and that his mother died of AIDS after being brutally raped. Do you know how that information was obtained?"

"UN and government officials interviewed the villagers to try to find out if there were parents alive or relatives who might take the children. There is a record of his father's death, and apparently, they spoke to a cousin of Yonas's mother who confirmed that she is dead. She is the only relative of the mother who is known to be alive, and she had three children of her own to raise and had no interest in adding Yonas to her brood."

"Do you have the name of the cousin or any way we can get in touch with her?" asked Heather.

"It wasn't in my original records, but I did make a few inquiries. After calling in some favors, I do have a name for you."

"That's wonderful news," said Madge.

"I hope it does not lead to disappointment. The information is a little old and the cousin may not be alive, or may be very reluctant to talk, but I wish you well."

As they headed back to their hotel, Heather and Madge made arrangements to visit the village where Yonas was born and see if they could find the cousin or anyone who knew Yonas's family. They were exhausted when they got back and had a quick dinner and headed to their rooms early. Tomorrow would be a long day.

~~~~~~

It was a three-hour drive to the village. They had a local driver and a guide who knew the area and could translate. They had a second car with the two security people Jason had insisted accompany them at all times.

The guide had suggested they stay in their vehicles while he made inquiries about the cousin. The job was made easier by handing out money Madge had given him for the villagers in exchange for information. About an hour later, he returned. "Come, I have found the cousin."

They walked on foot with the villagers staring at these strange American women and made their way to a small hut. A weary-looking woman of indeterminate age ushered them in and shooed children and a couple of chickens out the door.

The guide explained to her why they were there. She looked at Madge and Trish suspiciously, but when Madge pulled out a picture of herself holding Yonas when he was about five, she nodded her head, and started to talk.
~~~~~~

She confirmed that Yonas's father had gone off to war and never returned. Yonas's mother had no means of support other than trading crafts she made at the market. One day as she was on her way to the market, she was brutally attacked and raped by a solider. She crawled back to her cousin's hut, who helped her, but in their village, women who were raped were shunned. She and Yonas were forced to live on the outskirts of the village, where her cousin would sneak out to occasionally bring them food. But then she got very sick, and that's when the cousin realized she had AIDS and took Yonas back into the village. She couldn't care for him and sent him to the orphans' hut where he lived with several other children.

Heather and Madge couldn't help but feel emotional as they heard the horrors of the story. "Please ask her how long it was before she died." said Madge.

The guide translated, and the cousin responded, sadly shaking her head.

"She said she's not sure. She would sneak out to bring her what little food she could, leaving it at the door, but afraid to go in. But one day she arrived, and the door was wide open with no sign of her cousin. And she never saw her again."

Madge gasped. "So, she doesn't actually know if her cousin died?"

"No, but she said it is not possible she could have lived. She was like a skeleton, and very, very ill. She also said to tell you she is happy to see that Yonas survived."

Madge thanked her for her time and made sure the guide gave her a generous amount of money that would hopefully help her and her children for a while. She would make sure when she returned home to set up regular payments. This was, after all, Yonas's family and one day she would bring him here.

On the way to the hotel, Heather tried to console Madge. "Listen, just because the cousin can't confirm an actual death doesn't mean Yonas's mother is alive. Chances of that are slim to nothing."

"That makes it even more imperative that we track down this woman who says she is his mother."

"Well, money talks," said Heather. "I think you need to be prepared to spread some more of it around and hopefully that will lead us to her."

~~~~~~

For the next three days Madge and Heather worked every contact they had. They knew the "mother" was being kept in a safe house and protected by lawyers who were acting in her "best" interest. Finally, after a great deal of money was exchanged through emissaries, a cloak-and-dagger meeting was set up for the next day at noon at an office building not too far from their hotel. They were told to come alone, and they would be provided a translator. They would have thirty minutes and that was it.

"Jason will kill me when he finds out we ditched the security people," Madge said to Heather as they hurried down an alleyway in the back of the store the security detail thought they were shopping in.

"I think we're here," said Heather after about fifteen minutes of twists and turns through various alleyways that finally took them to a commercial street where they found themselves in a front of an unassuming building. They buzzed and were soon escorted in by an older woman who led them up a
~~~~~~

stairway and into a small waiting room.

A few minutes later, a stout man in a suit and tie entered the room. "I am Ahmed Kassa, and I represent Yonas's mother, Zala. Let me bring you in and introduce you to her," he said in excellent English. "After you hear her story, you will know the truth."

He brought them into a small conference room where a very tiny, very nervous young woman sat at the end of the table.

"Let me call for some tea," he said. And soon the woman who had escorted them up the stairs had poured tea for everyone. The young woman had barely looked up.

"What would you like to ask my client?"

"Well, I understand she was very ill with AIDS and then one day she just disappeared from her village. I would like to know what happened and how she survived."

Ahmad said a few words to Zala, and then turned back to them. "She has given me permission to tell you her story."

"After the village shunned her, she became very ill and could no longer take care of her precious son. She asked her cousin to please take care of him. She became weaker and weaker because she had very little food, and one day she left the village in search of something to eat. She remembers feeling very faint. And then the next thing she remembered she was in a hospital. She had been rescued by nuns who were doing missionary work, and they brought her to the hospital. She had very high fevers for several days and was delusional. When she was well enough to leave, the sisters took her to their mission. It took months for her to get strong again."

"What did the hospital diagnose her with?" asked Madge.

"She had problems from her brutal attack and had developed many infections that left her very ill."

"With AIDS?" Madge asked again.

"No. No. Fortunately she was spared that. Many months later, she returned to her village to find Yonas. No one could tell her what happened to him. She has spent the past six years trying to find him. And now she has."

Madge was very moved by the story and found herself tearing up.

"She knows she cannot take care of her child the way rich Americans can. She loves him and knows he is better off with you. But she needs to be compensated for all her pain and heartache."

"Compensated? What type of compensation are you looking for?"

Ahmad rubbed his chin and paused. "I believe my client should be compensated two million dollars. She will go away quietly and sign over her son to you."

Madge managed to stay cool. "Well, I don't have access to that money here. I would have to go home and discuss it with my husband."

"As you wish, Mrs. Madison. But you have exactly ten days to wire the money to this account," he said as he handed her a piece of paper. "Or we will start very public proceedings to have her son returned to her. As you know, my country no longer allows foreign adoptions, so they will be very agreeable to supporting this action."

With that, Madge and Heather stood up. The older woman suddenly appeared again, and escorted Zala out a side door.

Ahmad walked with them to the waiting room.

"Mrs. Madison, I trust I will hear from you soon."

"Oh, excuse me," said Heather, "I left my bag in the conference room."

A few minutes later they were back on the street, where they were confronted by their security guys who had tracked Madge there on her phone.

Heather said to them quickly, "We need to get out of here."

After a strong lecture from the security guys, they were escorted back to the hotel and Heather joined Madge in her suite.

"Well, what did you think?" asked Madge.

"I think it was a crock and this is a ruse to shake you and Jason down for money. That woman never looked up at you. She was scared to death. And don't you think if she was the mother, she would have asked to see pictures of Yonas? And supposedly she went back to the village. Her cousin would have mentioned that, don't you think?"

"Yes, I agree. I was really buying into it for a while, until he got to the two million dollars. And I was trying to make eye contact with her, but there was none. But I have to find out. Even though he's a shark, she might be an innocent victim and actually be Yonas's mother."

"Well, my friend, let's head back home because as soon as we land, we can find out."

"What do you mean?"

And with that, Heather reached into her tote bag and pulled out the teacup Zala had been drinking from. "DNA, my friend, DNA."

CHAPTER 22
WEDDING PLANS AND ANSWERS

Suzy was enjoying every second of the ride out to the North Fork with her precious cargo chatting away in the back seat. She had told Ian she'd bring Elsa out with her, which saved Ian the trip. He always met Emily, Elsa's mom, in the city when he picked her up for the weekends. They were doing a great job of co-parenting and had remained friends. Suzy adored Emily too and it was a chance to catch up with her before she and Elsa headed out East.

She was really looking forward to spending time with Keri and Chris. She had seen Keri only briefly in the spring when she had a business trip in New York City. But she was feeling a little nervous about telling Keri about Devon. She tended to be judgmental and was very protective of her father's memory.

When she pulled into the driveway, she was happy to see they had already arrived. Keri heard the car pull up and bounded down the porch steps just in time to swoop up a very excited Elsa into her arms. "Aunt Keri, I missed you so much."

"Not as much as I missed you, sweet pea."

It warmed Suzy's heart to see the love between aunt and niece. *Keri will be a great mom one day too,* she thought.

Chris and Ian had followed Keri onto the porch, and as soon as Keri put Elsa down, she ran up the steps to greet her dad.

"How about a hug for your old mom now?" Suzy said as Keri embraced her.

Hugs were exchanged by all and they made their way into house. After everyone had settled their things in their rooms, they headed back out to the porch. Ian had wine for the adults and a Shirley Temple for Elsa, who wanted to know if it was made with "organtic" stuff.

They all laughed. "Yes, sweetie, I think your mom would approve."

"I haven't been here in years," Keri said, "and I barely remember what it looked like, but I just love everything Ian's done with the house. And it's so peaceful sitting on a porch in rocking chairs. I can totally picture looking out on vineyards from this porch. So, how's that going?"

Ian eagerly told them all about his vision for the vineyards and how he was so fortunate to be learning the business from one of Mom's old friends who owned one of the top vineyards in the area.

Keri and Chris listened and asked great questions too.

"Well, little brother, you've grown up from that scrawny little brat to quite the entrepreneur," Keri said laughingly.

"Daddy was a brat?" Elsa piped in.

"I'm only teasing. I'm actually very proud of your dad. Cheers, little brother," Keri said and clinked glasses with Ian.

"Clink with me too," Elsa said as she raised her little Shirley Temple glass.

"So, Mom, who is this old friend Devon?"

Before Suzy could answer Ian replied, "Actually you'll get to meet him tonight. I invited him to dinner."

Suzy then added, "And if you're interested, tomorrow we can do a tour of his vineyard. They do a lot of weddings and it might be a lovely venue for you and Chris to think about."

~~~~~~

Devon arrived around six and brought some of his award-winning cabernets to go with the steaks that Ian and Chris were grilling up for dinner. They all enjoyed a glass of his cab on the porch while Devon charmed everyone with some of the local history of the North Fork.

"Well, I have to start preparing the steaks," said Ian.

Chris offered to help, and Suzy excused herself too. "I'm the salad maker."

"And I'm a salad maker," said Elsa as she skipped along happily into the house with her grandma.

"Tell me how you know my mom?" asked Keri.

"She was part of a group of summer kids who used to hang out with some of us local kids when we were growing up. Although I was a little older than your mom, so I didn't get to know her much until she was a little older."

"So, did you stay in touch through the years?"

"Not really. She went off to college around the time I graduated from college and got married. We lost touch, and I hadn't seen her until your aunt died. That's when I met Ian and it's been great getting to know him."

And then in an attempt to change the conversation, Devon continued, "Your brother says you're thinking of having your
~~~~~~

wedding out here next spring. I'll look forward to showing you around our vineyard tomorrow, although there are several other vineyards that also do weddings," he said as he stood up. "Let's see if they need some help with dinner, or someone to pour the wine."

Later that night as Suzy had just climbed into bed, Devon called to say what a lovely evening it had been with her family. "But when are you going to tell Keri about us? I was getting the third degree."

"I'm sorry to put you in that awkward situation. I just wanted her to meet you first, but I promise I will tell her after we tour the vineyard tomorrow."

~~~~~~

Keri and Chris were enthralled as they toured Martinique and later sat in the tasting room with Suzy, Devon, and the vineyard's wedding event planner. She told them they were usually booked at least a year in advance but as it happened, she just got a cancellation for Memorial Day weekend. They all agreed that would be perfect.

"If the weather cooperates, we can set everything up in tents," she said showing them photos of past weddings. "And our backup is always our beautiful and spacious tasting room."

As Keri and Chris perused the photos and asked questions, Devon excused himself. "I have some work to catch up on in the office, but, Suzy, let me know when you're finished, and I'll join you back here. We can sample some of the wines that are usually favorites at weddings."

About an hour later, the event planner left to put a folder together along with a proposal based on their discussion.
~~~~~~

"What do you think?" asked Suzy.

"Oh, Mom, I think it's just perfect," Keri gushed and Chris agreed too.

"That makes me so happy. I know it would have pleased Aunt Millie and my parents for you to be married on the North Fork. And of course, your dad," she said with a catch her throat. "Let me find Devon, and you and Chris can discuss this together."

Suzy found her way to Devon's office. The door was open and he motioned to her to come in as he quickly finished a call he was on.

"Well, what's the verdict?"

"They love it, and after they review the final proposal, it looks like we'll be having a wedding here."

"That's great news. Let's go out to the tasting room and I'll bring out those wines I promised. But first," he said as he took her into his arms, "I've been wanting to kiss you since you arrived today," and as their lips met, Suzy dissolved in his embrace.

They made their way back to the tasting room and Devon ordered flights of wine for them to try. Keri and Chris were delighted with everything.

It was now late afternoon, and Suzy reminded them that they needed to be heading home where they could relax a little before dinner. "I think you'll like the restaurant on the docks tonight, and they also serve Devon's wines there too." And then as casually as she could, she said, "Oh, and, Devon, you're welcome to join us."

They had barely pulled out of the vineyard when Keri turned to her mother. "Mom, I can't believe you didn't tell me you're in a relationship with Devon, or whatever it is," Keri said in that accusatory tone she had taken with Suzy ever since Ken had died.

"I-I..." Suzy started to stutter.

"And don't try to lie to me. I saw you in an embrace in his office when I was looking for the ladies' room."

"Keri, I had planned to tell you tonight. I just wanted you to meet him first and get to know him a little bit," Suzy said, almost on the verge of tears.

And then suddenly, Keri broke out in a huge smile. "Mom, I'm just busting your chops. Actually, I really like him. So now, tell us all the details."

Suzy signed with relief. "Well, let's get back to the farmhouse and I'll tell you all about it." *Well, at least most of it.* She left out the pregnancy and abortion. She had shared that with Ian in the context of what he was going through, but she saw no good reason to share that with Keri.

"So, how serious is this, Mom?"

"You know, I'm just taking it one day at a time. It's comforting to be with someone you knew long ago, but we're also different people now. And I still grieve for your father. But, Devon, does make me happy, and he makes me laugh, and that's something I wasn't sure would ever happen again."

Keri got up and put her arms around her mother. "You deserve to be happy, Mom. Dad would have wanted that. But it's just so hard to think about getting married without him to walk me down the aisle." And with that they both dissolved into tears.

"Grandma, Aunt Keri...why are you sad?" a little voice said behind them.

"Oh, honey, these are happy tears because your Aunt Keri is getting married."

"Yes," said Keri, wiping her eyes. "And you get to be my flower girl."

"Yippee," Elsa said jumping up and down with excitement. "What's a flower girl?"

She and Keri laughed as Keri explained to Elsa the role of a flower girl. "Can Bitania be one too?"

"Of course, sweet pea."

Suzy sat back and just smiled. *I think things will be okay.*

~~~~~~

Jason, Madge, and Heather had waited anxiously in Jason's office for the phone to ring with the results of the DNA test. After what seemed like an eternity, Jason's phone beeped.

"Yes, yes. Are you absolutely sure?" he paused. "Thanks for rushing this."

"There's no match."

"Oh, thank God," said Madge as she slowly sat down on the couch in Jason's office. "So, what do we do now?"

"We go through diplomatic channels and we report the lawyer for extortion."

Madge and Heather looked at each other.

"Jason, before we do that, we have to find this young woman. If he and whoever else is behind this knows we're coming after him, they'll kill her."

"She's right," said Heather. "We need to put people on this who can find her and protect her."

"All right, but this has to be done quickly."

Within an hour calls had been made and people on the ground were searching for the young woman.

Two days later, the body of an unidentified young wom-
~~~~~~

an was found dead in an alleyway. Madge and Heather were able to confirm from the gruesome photos that it was indeed the woman who had claimed to be Yonas's mother. They were further told by the authorities that there was no record of a lawyer by the name he had given Madge, and they considered the extortion case and the contested adoption closed.

Later that day the Ethiopian ambassador to the U.S. put out a statement that his government had investigated the illegal adoption claims and found them to be untrue and that Senator Madison and his wife had gone through all the proper legal channels to adopt their children.

That night, as she was ensconced in Jason's arms, Madge couldn't help but feel sad.

"I am so relieved that Yonas's adoption can't be contested, but I can't help feeling that I should have done more for the young woman they duped into doing this."

"Madge, you did everything you could," Jason said as he held her closer.

"I suppose, but her frightened young face will haunt me forever."

CHAPTER 23

OUT IN THE OPEN

It was a beautiful October evening. The trio had decided to have their martini meetup before their Ripe Tomatoes' dinner on the sidewalk at Café Fiorello across from Lincoln Center, a perfect spot for people watching.

"Well, here's a much-needed cheers that the adoption nightmare is over," said Suzy as they lifted their glasses and clinked.

"Thanks to you two for being my rocks as this was unfolding," said Madge. "I don't know what I would have done without you."

"Do you think you'll ever find out if Senator Delano was behind any of this?" asked Trish.

"My gut says yes. Heather has a couple of investigative reporters digging into it, but I think it's doubtful we'll turn up any evidence. And while we're talking about Heather, she has been amazing through all of this. It's hard to believe we were once 'rivals.' And if Heather hadn't had the courage to come forward against the predator who ran our TV news network when we were both there, he'd still be preying on women."

"Yes," said Suzy, "but if you hadn't backed her up with your own story no one would have believed her. And you both came forward before the 'Me Too' movement became a movement, in no small measure because you both took a stand."

"And if that happened now, he wouldn't have just left the network in disgrace, he'd be sitting in a prison cell instead of one of his three mansions," Madge added.

"Well, here's to the good guys like Jason. Let's hope this election proves that good guys can win," said Trish.

They all clinked glasses again.

~~~~~~

The Ripe Tomatoes had settled into their usual round table. Everyone was elated that the adoption scandal had been put to rest, and they were all actively campaigning for Jason.

Arlene had hosted several events in Sag Harbor over the summer. Celeste and her husband Sir Oliver had hosted events in Celeste's New York City apartment with some of New York's most prominent philanthropists. Trish had courted some of Harlem's community leaders and activists who had met with Jason and become strong supporters.

Madge looked around the table at this beautiful group of ageless women, whose true beauty came from within. They exuded a confidence that comes only with age—having lived a life of ups and downs, of sorrows and joys, mistakes and failures, triumphs and successes to finally become comfortable in who they are. Of course, that didn't mean that petty rivalries ceased, or old wounds were healed, as Hope was about to prove when Celeste asked her how the show was going.

"The previews are going well, and ticket sales are strong.
~~~~~~

We're doing little tweaks here and there, but that bitch Ellen is still leaking stories to the press that continually put me a bad light," said Hope. "The latest story is that I disrupt rehearsals with ridiculous suggestions for last-minute changes to the show. Of course, she continues to deny it's her. We don't even speak now, so we'll have to put on quite a Tony-winning performance as 'best friends' for our after-party on opening night."

Suzy gingerly asked the next question, "Hope, have you considered that maybe it's not her, and that someone else is trying to drive a wedge between the two of you and cause havoc with the show?" Everyone held their breath waiting for Hope's reaction, although Suzy always had a way of calming Hope when no one else could.

Hope seemed to be taking in Suzy's words, and after a long pause, said, "You know it's hard for me to admit when I'm wrong, and I would gladly be wrong on this one, but I don't think I am."

That was their cue to move on to other topics, and this was the night Suzy had decided to tell the group about Keri's wedding and Devon.

"I have exciting news. Keri and Chris are getting married this spring and I hope you will all be there."

"Oh, how wonderful, and where will it be?" asked Celeste.

"Actually, that's the second part of my exciting news." Then she told them about Devon (the public version) and that Keri's wedding would in the vineyard he owns.

Suzy laughed as they all started asking questions at the same time, but she didn't mind answering (at the least the ones she wanted to answer) because she knew how genuinely happy they all were for her.

When Suzy got back to the apartment, she called Devon. "We're out in the open now, and I hope you're ready for this." Then she told him how excited her friends were.

"I'm looking forward to meeting all of them."

"Watch what you wish for," she said laughingly.

~~~~~~

Suzy wasn't used to being a lady of leisure, and still got up at six every morning and headed to the gym in her building. She had just returned to the apartment when her cell rang. It was Amy.

"Have you looked at The Three Tomatoes website lately?"

Suzy had deliberately tried to keep away from it, and with everything that was going on in her life, it had been fairly simple.

"No, why?"

"They've gone full-on thirtysomething with articles like How to Tell Your Best Friend Her Husband's on Bumble and When to Make the Decision to Freeze Your Eggs. But you have to read the comments. These are our subscribers and they're mad as hell."

"I'll look right now and then I'll call you back."

Amy was right. This wasn't a website that was trying to broaden its base. It was narrowing it and excluding the very women that were The Three Tomatoes's core audience. And they were angry.

I'm canceling my subscription!

*I want **my** Three Tomatoes.*

Did we suddenly become invisible again?

There were hundreds of comments posted under the vari-
~~~~~~

ous articles.

Suzy called Amy back.

"And wait 'til you see the comments on Facebook and Instagram," said Amy. "And subscribers are tweeting you, Trish, and Madge begging you to bring back their Three Tomatoes. I think there's a revolt underway."

"I think you're right, Amy, but our hands are tied."

"So, you're just going to let them destroy what we all worked so hard to build over the past five years?"

"Amy, believe me, I'm just as upset about this as you are. I just need a little time to absorb this."

Suzy opened her Twitter feed. The Three Tomatoes was now one of the trending topics with #IWantMyThreeTomatoes.

CHAPTER 24
#IWANTMYTHREETOMATOES

Within two weeks, the rallying cry #IWantMyThreeTomatoes was still trending on social media, including a Facebook group that now numbered in the thousands. It was through that group that the idea of a protest in front of North Star's corporate headquarters sprang to life with a call to women over forty across the country to join them the following Wednesday in protest.

Heather called Madge and told her that her network's local station would be covering it, and she was certain the others would too.

Suzy, Trish, Madge, and Amy made plans to meet at the loft penthouse to watch the coverage. Since the protest was taking place in the morning, they figured the networks would cover it during their midday news broadcasts.

The teaser at the top of the news was Grandmas Protest at North Star's Headquarters.

"Grandmas?" said Madge. "Well, we know where this is going."

It was covered at the very end of the news by a twenty-something guy reporter.

"Looks like several hundred angry older women are protesting the editorial changes on a digital publication called The Three Tomatoes that use to cater to the silver-haired grannies and is now targeting a younger audience." He then walked over with his mic to a group of very attractive middle-aged women who looked like they could be the reporter's older sisters, not his grandmother. "So, what's this protest all about?" he asked pointing the mic to one of them.

"It's about not being fucking invisible to fucking corporate assholes," she said before he quickly removed the mic just in time to bleep her.

"Well, there you have it," he said, as the camera cut away.

They stood there just looking at each other.

"Well, is anyone surprised by that coverage?" asked Suzy rhetorically.

"I'm seething, but not surprised. It's the whole reason we started The Three Tomatoes in the first place—to change the perceptions of older women as angry and bitter hags," said Madge.

"And to give us a voice," added Trish.

As they were talking, Amy was on her cell, and then turned to them. "That was a friend at the NYPD. He said there were at least three thousand women there this morning. So much for the 'few hundred' bullshit. So, what do we do?"

They sat there gloomily.

Then Suzy spoke. "Well, if we had the money and North Star was willing, we could buy their shares back."

"Those are a lot of big *ifs,"* said Trish with a huge sigh.

"And if Jason wasn't running for the senate, we could front the money for a buyback, but we can't own a media company now."

"There's only one thing we can do," said Suzy.

They all looked at her.

"Let's treat ourselves to lunch at Balthazar's and eat their decadent desserts."

And off they went.

~~~~~~

Suzy hadn't seen Margot Tuttinger in weeks, but rang her on the off chance that she might have returned from wherever her wanderlust was taking her these days. She was pleasantly surprised when Margot answered.

"I only just returned from Tahiti, and yes I'd love to have dinner and catch up on everything that's happened since I've been gone. Let's go to my favorite little neighborhood French bistro."

They were shown to Margot's favorite table immediately and the maître d' welcomed her back with open arms. He then brought over her favorite red wine. "Our gift to have you back," he said.

Over wine and a wonderful meal, Margot shared her latest travel adventures. When Suzy shared her news about Devon, Keri's upcoming wedding, and the vineyard that Ian was starting, Margot sat back with her legendary poker face. And then she broke out in a smile. "How extraordinary. I've been gone for only a few weeks and look at all the wonderful things that are happening in your life. My dear, I could not be happier for you. And I do want to meet this Devon person. You know he must meet with my seal of approval," she said with a smile. But Suzy realized then how much her seal of approval would
~~~~~~

mean to her.

"That's all the good stuff," Suzy continued. "And since you've been out of the country you probably haven't heard any of the news on The Three Tomatoes front." Suzy filled her in.

"I can't say I'm surprised. This is so typical. Big companies buying a brand that's doing well and then trying to make it into something it isn't and totally screwing it up. Arpello Perfume is a classic example."

"Needless to say, we're all upset to see this happening to our baby that we worked so hard to grow and flourish. If there was some way we could get it back we would," said an emotional Suzy.

After a few moments of silence, Margot said, "Perhaps there is a way. Give me a few days and we'll talk again.

~~~~~~

It was opening night of Hope's Broadway show. Devon came into New York for the big event, which would also be his debut to the Ripe Tomatoes who would all be there.

Suzy put the finishing touches on her hair and walked into the living room, where she was greeted with a whistle from Devon.

"You look sexy as hell."

And she did, in a simple knitted black dress that hugged her curves in all the right places and stopped a few inches above her knees. Her beautiful long legs looked even longer in her three-inch Manolos. One of the benefits of being underemployed was she had more time for long walks in Central Park and Pilates and yoga classes.

"And you look very dashing. The Tomatoes will fall in love
~~~~~~

with you just like I have."

As they made their way into the theater lobby, Suzy spotted Arlene and Bill chatting with Celeste and Sir Oliver, and she and Devon joined them.

After introductions and a brief chat, they headed into the theater to their seats next to Jason and Madge. Trish and Michael were just in front of them.

The excitement of opening night filled the air. People were in the aisles chatting as they spotted friends everywhere like it was a cocktail party, while ushers tried politely to get everyone seated.

Madge whispered to Suzy, "How nervous do you think Hope is right now?"

And then the music started, and the audience was soon caught up in the life story of an iconic female rock star of the 1980s, the acting, the singing, the costumes, and the music they all knew so well from their youth.

The standing ovation was spontaneous—not one of those were "plants" in the front rows who stand and everyone else feels obligated to stand too. This was the real deal.

They waited for the theater to empty and then walked to nearby Sardi's for the after-party.

"Well, I'm looking forward to a wonderful celebratory evening," said Celeste. "How many times have we been to the after-party of a show that's been a disaster and it's like attending a wake? And with all the drama leading up to this one, it could have been just that. I think the gossip mongers will have to eat a lot of crow."

They all agreed. "And maybe this will help mend the feud between Hope and Ellen," Trish the eternal optimist added.

Suzy nodded, but she wasn't at all sure about that.

Sardi's was packed with the usual opening night crowd. Celebrities, politicians, the 1 percenters, press, the show's investors, and friends of the producers and the cast.

Ellen was holding court in the center of the room, but they still hadn't seen any sign of Hope. Then again, she did love grand entrances. Twenty minutes later, she did not disappoint.

Suddenly the room was buzzing as Hope entered, locked arm in arm with the beautiful star of the show—so much for that supposed feud. They were encircled immediately, and Ellen was left standing in the proverbial dust.

Suzy, Trish, and Madge raised their eyebrows at each other with that "leave it to Hope" bemused look.

With Devon's arm around her waist, Suzy started making the rounds to introduce him to some of the people she knew. She loved how Devon handled himself in every situation with charm and grace.

They were in the back of the room when glasses started to tinkle signaling that the remarks were about to start. The director and the cast were at the front of the room with Ellen and Hope on opposite ends.

The director spoke and thanked the wonderful cast to huge applause from everyone in the room, and then asked Ellen and Hope to say a few words from their opposing corners. It was as if a cold arctic air had just blown through the room, but each kept her remarks short and sweet.

Suzy let out a little sigh of relief, and then out of the corner of her eye, she spotted a face she knew. She glanced over and realized it was Ellen's ex-husband, and he was standing next to one of the tabloid gossip columnists who had printed several of the unflattering stories about Hope from anonymous sources. And that was the moment Suzy knew who was planting all those stories.

As the party was winding down, she and Devon said their goodbyes, and Suzy whispered to Trish and then Madge that she knew who the gossip culprit was. "We'll talk in the morning," she whispered.

~~~~~~

"Do you really have to leave so early?" Suzy said to Devon as they untangled themselves from their passionate lovemaking.

"You little minx," he said nuzzling her neck. "Believe me, I wish we could stay in bed all day, but I do have to get back to the vineyard."

"Well, let me at least make you a quick breakfast while you shower."

Fifteen minutes later they were seated at the little bistro table in Suzy's kitchen. "I could get use to this," Devon said as he ate scrambled eggs. Suzy smiled in agreement.

"And that was quite the story about Ellen's ex-husband. Your theory is very plausible."

When they had returned home from Sardi's, Suzy told Devon about the bitter divorce Ellen and her husband went through. They had been producing partners for many years and had made a ton of money too. They had the prewar apartment on Park Avenue and a beautiful home in the Hamptons. They seemed to have it all until the day Ellen came home unexpectedly and found him in bed with the male star of their latest show.

Ellen went for the jugular. She hired the top divorce attorney in New York City and by the time she finished he was
~~~~~~

lucky to have enough money to keep a roof over his head. And it seems Ellen was the one with the talent for raising money for a show and her ex hadn't had a success since their divorce.

"So, when I saw him in the back of the room with the gossip columnist with that smug look on his face, I knew it had to be him," she told Devon.

After breakfast they said their reluctant goodbyes. "I'll see you in two very long days," Suzy said as she kissed him at the door.

She had just poured herself another cup of coffee when her phone buzzed. It was Trish, and as they started to talk, Madge called, so she conferenced them both into the call.

"You'd make quite the detective, Suzy Hamilton," Trish said laughingly when Suzy finished her story. Both she and Madge agreed that Suzy's instincts were spot-on.

"So, are you going to tell Hope?"

"Yes, I thought I'd see if she's free for lunch. The reviews are starting to come in and they're terrific. Even the gossip columnist loved the show, which she said is a success in spite of the 'dueling producers.' But hopefully she will be in a good mood even with that snide remark."

"Let us know how it goes," Madge said as they all signed off.

CHAPTER 25

MR. SENATOR

Madge had just come out of the bathroom wrapped in a fluffy white towel, into their spacious bedroom where Jason was standing in the walk-in closet, clad only in his boxer shorts, picking out a tie for the evening—and not just any evening, but election evening.

Madge watched him quietly for a moment. He still took her breath away, and she couldn't help thanking the universe for the umpteenth time for bringing Jason into her life.

She walked quietly into the walk-in closet and dropped the towel. "Need a little help with that, sailor?"

"I think I do, pretty lady. Do you pop into men's closets often?" he said lustily as he took her into his arms. Then Madge slowly started making her way down the front of his body with kisses until she was kneeling in front of his very erect manhood and encased him with her mouth. Jason groaned, and then slid onto the closet floor bringing Madge down on top of him where their passion quickly ignited into a crescendo of simultaneous climaxes.

They stayed on the floor for a few minutes as their passion

subsided. “That certainly released the tension,” Jason said in a husky voice.

Madge leaned over and kissed him. “Well, Mr. Senator, let’s find you a tie and get you erected, I mean elected.”

Their friends and family started to arrive at their Brooklyn brownstone around eight o’clock. The polls closed at 9:00 p.m. and they had set up TV monitors throughout the house so everyone could watch the election results. The polls all indicated a close race, so they could be looking at a long night, and possibly even recounts.

“Madge, you look so calm,” Suzy said as she followed her into the kitchen to see how she could help.

“You know, it’s strange. I feel calm too. At this point it’s out of our hands and the voters will make the decision.” She took Suzy’s hand and squeezed it. “And you know, either way we’ll be just fine.”

By 10:00 p.m. with about a hundred people crowded into their den, the networks called the election for Jason. They had tuned in to Heather Stone who was covering the results. “We’re expecting New York State Senator Frank Delano to concede shortly,” she said.

The house erupted in joy. Jason swept Madge into his arms and then turned for hugs with his beaming parents. Yonas and Bitania, who had been allowed to stay up way past their bedtimes, were so excited they were leaping all over their dad.

Jason made his way through the house hugging his friends and family, until finally his campaign manager reminded him they needed to get to campaign headquarters so Jason could make his acceptance speech and thank his supporters.

Campaign headquarters was pandemonium. The local

networks were all covering the event. The next day Jason's eloquent remarks calling for party unity, and his pledge to work for the people of New York, not the lobbyists and special interest groups, had made national news. He was being called the rising star of his party, and Vegas was already laying odds on his being his party's next presidential candidate.

Jason and Madge had been devouring the election coverage. "They're already talking about you for the next presidential race."

"That's just the talking heads being talking heads. I want to do the best job I can for the state of New York over the next six years. I'm so glad campaigning is over, and I have no interest in higher political office...that's not what we signed on for."

"Never say never," said Madge, realizing as smart and successful as her husband was, when it came to the game of politics, he was still a babe in the woods. She just hoped they wouldn't eat him alive.

~~~~~~

It was a few days before Thanksgiving and Suzy had invited her two best friends to her apartment for martinis before their Ripe Tomatoes dinner. For the first time in many years, they'd be separated for the holiday. Madge had invited them all to the farm in Vermont again, but Trish and Suzy had talked separately to each other and agreed that Madge and Jason really needed some quiet alone time with their family after their hectic and stressful year. Suzy and Ian were hosting Thanksgiving on Long Island and had invited Trish and Michael, but they had volunteered to serve meals in Harlem this year.

"Suzy, this is wonderful, but you know we really could
~~~~~~

have had our martinis at a bar," Madge said looking at the beautiful display of crudités and the spectacular charcuterie board Suzy had put together herself.

"Well, in between seething over what the corporate idiots are doing to The Three Tomatoes, I have time on my hands. And I wanted the three of us to have a little quiet time especially since we won't be spending Thanksgiving together. Plus, I have a little gift for both of you and you'll be relieved to know it's not handmade. I haven't gone full-on Martha Stewart yet." And with that she presented each of them with an iconic blue Tiffany box.

Trish and Madge looked at her in surprise.

"Well, don't just sit there, go ahead and open them."

Inside each box was a beautiful delicate eighteen-carat rose gold bracelet with a small round brilliant diamond. As they lifted the bracelets out of the boxes, they exclaimed *you shouldn't haves*, along with, *this is so beautiful.*

"Suzy, it's not even anyone's birthday, and Christmas is more than a month away."

"It's just a little gift to tell you how much I love you both, and without your love and support I could never have gotten through the past year and a half since Ken died. When I think back to last Thanksgiving in Vermont, where I was just going through the motions of living, I'm so grateful that this year I have so many things to be thankful for, and you two are at the top of that list," Suzy said as she started to tear up.

And then they all teared up.

"Here's to us," said Suzy as she lifted her martini glass, "and to everlasting friendship."

~~~~~~
~~~~~~

As the trio headed to their usual table for the Ripe Tomatoes' dinner, they almost stopped short. Seated next to Hope was none other than Ellen and she appeared to be laughing at something Hope had just said. *Wonders will never cease,* thought Suzy as they were seated.

Nearly all the Ripe Tomatoes were there—Celeste, looking elegantly beautiful, Arlene whose fashion sense never failed, Heather who even in her black Armani anchor uniform still looked sexy, Miriam who looked like she might have had another face-lift, and of course larger-than-life Hope who was wearing a bold statement necklace and her oversize sunglasses. As Suzy looked around the table she was once again in awe of this amazing group of stunning, smart, accomplished women who were far more interesting and engaging now than they were in their twenties and thirties. *We do get better*, Suzy thought, which made her even more determined to find a way to get The Three Tomatoes back.

Once their drinks arrived, Hope took center stage and lifted her glass. "Well, Tomatoes, I am happy to welcome Ellen into our Ripe Tomatoes fold."

They clinked glasses in cheers.

Celeste was the first to speak up. "Welcome, Ellen! We are delighted to have another lovely Tomato in our little coterie. But I must ask what we are all no doubt thinking, how the hell did this happen?" she said with that throaty laugh of hers.

Hope and Ellen then told the group how Suzy figured out the culprit. When she and Ellen cornered the gossip columnist who had spread most of the unfounded tales, she didn't confirm, but didn't deny that it was Ellen's ex.

"Our lawyers sent him a strongly written letter threatening him with a libel suit, which seems to have put the pin in him. Now Ellen and I can finally enjoy the success of our wonderful new show, and fingers crossed, maybe even a Tony win together. And we're looking at our next production."

That prompted more cheers.

They went around the table catching up on everyone's news. Celeste's latest book had already hit the best-seller list; Miriam had a new boyfriend, several years her junior (explaining the latest face-lift); Arlene and Bill were still very much a couple; and Heather bemoaned that she had no time for a social life, and the Tomatoes' dinners were one of her rare fun things to do.

"I am very grateful for this group of kind, supportive, and fun women," Heather said.

"I couldn't agree more," added Celeste. "We all have much to be grateful for and I am thankful for another wonderful dinner with my beautiful friends."

They parted ways with hugs and well wishes for Thanksgiving.

CHAPTER 26
ANOTHER THANKSGIVING

Ian was excited to be preparing his very first Thanksgiving dinner. Suzy was in awe watching him do his preparations in the kitchen, just like she used to watch his father.

"How can I help?"

"Well, Mom, after hearing for years how you left the plastic package inside the bird and practically burned the kitchen down when you and Dad first got married, I think you can just sit back and drink wine," he laughed. "And let's face it, Mom, you have lots of talents, but cooking was never one of them."

"And I'm glad I inherited Mom's noncooking skills," said Keri entering the kitchen. "So, I'll just drink wine too."

Suzy and Keri were soon caught up in wedding conversation, as Ian chopped, diced, and stuffed the bird.

"I'm so happy that we now have our Memorial Day weekend date, and we'll send out save the date cards soon. And, Mom, I can't wait to look at gowns with you this week."

"Oh, Keri, nothing will make me happier. Arlene was great and got us appointments with some wonderful wedding gown designers, and she knows them all."

Devon joined them for dinner later that afternoon. Suzy felt grateful looking around the table at her wonderful children, and her soon to be son-in-law, and she was thankful that they had all accepted Devon too. But she knew she had to make a special toast this year.

"I could never have imagined last Thanksgiving that I would be sitting in Aunt Millie's dining room grateful for so many things that this past year has brought us. We have a wedding to celebrate, Ian's vineyard to look forward to, and the surprise of having Devon back in my life.

"But we also have an empty place at our table that can never be filled. Thanksgiving was always Ken's favorite day and without him it was a day I was dreading again this year. But being here right now with all of you, I know that Ken is looking down on us and that he's smiling. He would have wanted us to go on. So, let's raise our glasses to Ken, a loving husband and wonderful dad, who will live forever in our hearts."

Keri and Suzy had agreed to clean up after dinner since Ian, with help from Chris and Devon, had done all the cooking. As Suzy brought the dishes into the kitchen, she looked on the windowsill, and there was a cardinal, peering back at her.

~~~~~~

The following day, Ian suggested they all go for a long bike ride. Suzy declined because she was meeting Devon at his beach house for lunch.

The air was brisk, but it was sunny and there were still some colorful fall leaves on the trees. When she arrived, Devon led her up to the second level of the beach house with its
~~~~~~

beautiful view of the water, which they paid no attention to as their clothes went flying off and Devon was soon pleasuring Suzy with his tongue. She grasped the top of his head as his tongue and fingers glided in and out of her until she was soon crying out in ecstasy. Then he slipped inside her, and before long she was riding a second wave of passion.

They collapsed alongside each other, lulled to sleep now by the sound of the waves lapping against the beach.

Suzy opened her eyes as Devon, who had quietly showered and dressed, gently kissed her on the lips.

"Well, Suzy Sunshine, relax, shower, and then come downstairs for lunch."

"Sounds good even though I thought I'd never eat again after yesterday's feast."

She showered, picked up her clothes that were strewn around, dressed, pulled her hair into a ponytail, and headed downstairs. "Thanks for making a salad. I don't think I can look at another piece of turkey again...until at least tomorrow. So now, tell me your news. You've kept me in suspense all week."

"You know that Carol and I co-own the vineyard that she has never really had any interest in running. I've been thinking for a long time about buying her out, and now especially with you in my life, I'd really like to make a clean break with her. She's agreed and she's coming back from Paris next week to sign the papers."

"Devon, that's a huge step. Are you sure about this?"

"I've never been surer of anything."

~~~~~~
~~~~~~

Trish and Michael spent the better part of Thanksgiving Day serving meals at one of the local churches in Harlem. When Trish looked around at all the people enjoying their dinners at the festively decorated tables, it broke her heart that if not for places like these, most of these people might not have had any meal today. It was especially heartbreaking to see mothers and their children here.

Later that evening as she and Michael were enjoying a wonderful Thanksgiving meal at Red Rooster Harlem, Trish had mixed feelings.

"You know, Michael, we are so blessed. Here we are eating dinner at a four-star restaurant in a neighborhood where many don't have enough to eat, or don't have access to decent health care or jobs."

"I know, I had the same thought."

"I've been thinking, now that we are part of this community, we need to do more than just be a business owner here. Maybe we could start doing some free programs at the gallery that might help people. I could start a series of healthy living programs that would educate people on issues like the health problems with obesity, healthy eating, and exercise."

"That's a great idea, Trish, and it gets you back into an area that you are so passionate about, and one that helped grow The Three Tomatoes too. And you know, maybe I could offer a series of courses on how to start a business, and maybe even find some funding for people with good ideas."

They talked well into the evening, and the more they talked, the more excited they got. By the end of the weekend, they had put together a proposal of ideas that Trish suggested they share with some of the community leaders for input.

~~~~~~

It was the day after Thanksgiving, and Jason and Madge were sitting out by the firepit enjoying a glass of wine. Jason's parents had taken the kids to visit his sister Chrissy's nearby horse farm.

"As much as I love Trish and Suzy, I'm glad we're able to have a quiet weekend with just our little family," said Madge. "It's been quite a year, and it's good to just chill."

"I couldn't agree more. And now that the election is over and the adoption issue is in the past, I hope we can settle into a new routine where I can be senator, husband, and dad in a much more balanced way than I have in the past few months. It hasn't escaped me that you've been spending all your time campaigning and being mom and dad to the kids too."

"We'll figure it out," Madge said assuredly. "And actually, after traveling the state and listening to people's concerns these past few months, I have been thinking about a new documentary."

"That's great. What would the focus be?"

"It would be about how and why underserved communities get inferior education, health care, food sources, and much more. It would shine a light on the inequalities between the haves and the have-nots on these basic rights, and what we can do about it."

Jason leaned over to Madge and gave her a long kiss. "There are so many ways I love you, Madge Thompson Madison, that I've lost count of them."
~~~~~~

CHAPTER 27

THE PERFECT GOWN AND HATCHED PLANS

Suzy and Keri had spent Monday and Tuesday visiting designers' showrooms. It was Tuesday afternoon when they visited the last one before Keri had to get the shuttle back to Boston. And that was where the magic happened. In each of the other lavish showrooms they were presented with several styles by often effusive salespeople who thought that just "every gown," ridiculously overpriced, would be perfect for Keri. But the last one was different.

They rang the buzzer at one of the old apartment buildings with railroad flats in the East Village. They walked up to the second floor where they were greeted by the designer, a young up-and-comer who was generating a lot of buzz. She sat and talked with Keri for half an hour. Everything from what she did for work, what she did for fun, her style preferences, and how she pictured herself on her wedding day. And then, instead of pulling out a host of gowns, she said quietly, "I think I might have the gown for you."

She came back a few minutes later with a sample gown

that had been worn only once on a runway. "Try it on. You're model-thin and about the same height as the model who wore it." Then she turned to her seamstress and asked her to help Keri into the gown.

Ten minutes later, Keri walked back into the studio. Suzy took one look at her and started to cry. And then Keri started to cry. And then the designer cried.

"This is the most perfect dress," Keri said elatedly, between tears.

"And it fits you like a dream too," said Suzy.

"We can make a few alterations here and there, but yes, I think it's perfect too," said the designer.

While Suzy had been prepared to pay an outrageous amount of money for a designer gown that would be worn one time, the best part was that the designer sold it to them for a fraction of the cost because it was a sample.

"This was the best day ever," Keri said as she hugged her mother before jumping in an Uber and heading to LaGuardia. Suzy's heart swelled with love.

As she headed back up to her apartment, her phone pinged. It was Margot texting to see if she was free for dinner.

At seven o'clock they were back at Margot's favorite bistro. Margot got right to the point.

"Suzy, I've been doing some digging behind the scenes at The Three Tomatoes. It's turning into a disaster. Not only have they lost their core subscriber base of women over forty-five, but they're also not attracting all those new younger subscribers they had hoped for. There's a lot of competition for that audience and they don't seem to be striking a chord with them. And of course, as a result, their ad revenues are way down too."

Suzy looked at her in amazement. "How did you get all that info?"

"I have my sources," said Margot slyly.

"Well, in other breaking news," said Suzy, "Amy heard from some of our former employees who were all let go within the past two months. All of them over forty-five while younger employees stayed. They're about to file a class action age discrimination suit."

"Oh, that's wonderful news," said Margot, almost giddy with joy.

"How is that wonderful?"

"It means they'll be ripe for a buyback."

"That's interesting, but who would buy them?"

"You would, of course."

"Margot, I've already told you none of us are in a position to do that right now."

"I know, dear, but I am. Here's how it would work." Over dinner and wine, Margot laid out her plan.

Suzy was so excited by the proposal that on her way home in an Uber she texted Trish, Madge, and Amy to meet her the following day at the loft.

~~~~~~

Suzy laid out Margot's strategy and proposition. They would give The Three Tomatoes until January to drop into even more of a slump, and then Margot would call the chairman of North Star, whom she serves with on some prestigious nonprofit boards, and make him an offer to "unload" The Three Tomatoes and the negative press.

"Her offer will be significantly below what they paid for
~~~~~~

the company. And she will put up the money for the buyback. She said now that she's traveled the world, taken painting lessons, writing lessons, and read all the latest best sellers, she is ready to get back in the game," Suzy explained.

"She'll be chairman, and we will all be given shares in the company in exchange for rebuilding the brand. Amy, she'd like you to take the reins as CEO again with a generous salary, and each of us will receive consulting fees based on the level of involvement and time we can commit to getting our baby back up and running profitably. And we'd be the face of the company again for PR purposes. So, who's in?"

They all sat there for a few minutes letting it sink in.

Trish was the first to leap up with a "Hell yes, I'm in," which was followed in kind by Madge and then Amy who was over the moon.

They talked over the details for the next couple of hours.

"Listen, Margot said we have to keep a tight lid on this. No one is to breathe a word to anyone, except to Michael and Jason. And their opinions will be most welcome," cautioned Suzy.

"Agreed," said Madge. "And it's not a deal 'til it's a done deal and there's lots that could still go wrong."

Trish, their optimist, was giddy with excitement. "I just know the stars will align."

They all went out to dinner, and afterwards Suzy went home and crawled into bed exhausted and happy. It had been quite a day. It wasn't until the next morning that she realized she hadn't heard from Devon.

~~~~~~
~~~~~~

She tried calling and texting him several times the next day. No response. This just wasn't like him.

On the following day when she hadn't heard from him, out of fear and panic, she called Ian.

"I'm sorry to bother you, but I'm worried sick. I haven't heard from Devon in over two days. Have you seen or heard from him?"

"Yeah. I saw him Monday night at A Lur Chowder House. He was having dinner with a dark-haired woman. I waved to him, but they were deep in conversation. I know you mentioned his ex-wife was coming to town, so I figured that was her, and I didn't want to disturb them."

"Well, thanks, sweetie. At least I know he's okay."

Suzy barely got through the rest of the day. *Something's wrong*. She couldn't stand the thought of being in the apartment a second longer and called Trish to see if she was free for dinner. Trish could tell by the tone of her voice that something was amiss.

"Of course, Suzy. Let's go someplace quiet. How about that little Italian restaurant near your apartment?"

When Trish arrived, she was escorted to a small corner table in the back of the restaurant. Thank goodness they were away from prying eyes because Suzy was a mess. She started crying the second Trish sat down.

"I haven't heard from him at all," she said between sobs and sips of wine. "I feel just like I did all those years ago when Carol suddenly came home that summer, and I didn't hear from him for days. And then when I did, it was to tell me he was marrying her. What if they're getting back together and he doesn't want to tell me?"

Trish tried to console Suzy as best she could. "Suzy, that

just doesn't make sense. Everyone can see how in love he is with you. And he's already told you what a loveless marriage it was. There must be something else going on. I'm sure it will be fine."

Suzy wasn't so sure. She went home and for the second night in a row she cried herself to sleep.

The next afternoon she got a call from Ian.

"Mom, I was supposed to have a meeting with Devon this afternoon in his office to discuss some of the plans for our vineyard. When I arrived, his assistant said he wasn't there and actually hadn't shown up the day before either. So, I immediately drove out to the beach house. His car was there, and I kept banging on the door and no one answered. Just as I was about to leave, he finally opened the door.

"He was totally shit-faced and looked like he'd hadn't changed his clothes in days. He mumbled that it wasn't a good time to talk, and everyone should just leave him the fuck alone."

Suzy was speechless. "Ian, I'm coming out right away to see him."

"Mom, no. I don't think you should do that. Whatever's going on with him he's going to have to deal with it alone. I'll keep an eye on him."

When she got off the phone with Ian, she called Trish.

"I have to agree with Ian. I don't think running out there is going to solve anything right now. Give it a couple of days. Should I come over?"

"No, Trish. I don't need a babysitter. But thanks." Then she realized how curt that sounded, and added, "Trish, I didn't mean it the way it sounded. I just need to be alone."

"Oh, Suzy, I understand. Just know I am here."

It was an agonizing week. On Friday she got a hand-delivered letter from Devon.

Dear Suzy,

Forgive me yet again for causing you pain. I have a lot to process right now, and I need to do that alone. You are the best woman I know, and I truly don't deserve you. When I'm in a better place, l will try to explain to you if you let me.

With all my heart, I love you.

Devon

Suzy cried for hours. And then she got angry. *I should never have trusted that man and I never will again.*

CHAPTER 28
A WAY BACK

It was the week before Christmas and Suzy had just left Margot's Fifth Avenue apartment. They had been meeting a couple of times a week with Amy to strategize the best way to bring The Three Tomatoes back, assuming they succeeded with the buyback plans. Suzy was grateful to have something other than Devon to focus on right now, but it wasn't easy because her heart felt ripped apart.

She decided to stroll down Fifth Avenue and try to find some Christmas spirit. She stopped to look at the beautifully decorated store windows as she made her way through the throngs to the tree at Rockefeller Center. She took in the sight of the lighted angels, and slowly made her way through the crowds to get up closer to see the tree. *It is magical,* she thought, as she watched the skaters on the rink. She was looking forward to bringing Elsa here to skate.

Then she made her way across the street to St. Patrick's Cathedral. She sat in a back pew, said a silent prayer, and had one of her many conversations with Ken. In the beginning they were angry conversations about why he had left them.

But with time, her talks were thankful for all the wonderful years they had together, and the memories cheered her more now than saddened her. Before she left, she lit a candle and said a prayer for all those she loved, including Devon.

She realized it was time to get her Christmas act together since Ian and Elsa were spending Christmas Eve with her. Two blocks from her apartment there was a sidewalk vendor selling trees, and she found one that would fit well in the living room. "Can you deliver this today?" she inquired.

"I can have it there in an hour," he replied.

When she got back to the apartment, she poured herself a glass of wine and then pulled out the boxes of Christmas lights, ornaments, and various decorations she had saved from the house. She decided she would put the tree up tonight with the lights, and then invite Trish and Madge over one night during the week to help her decorate it. She was starting to feel better already.

An hour later the tree was delivered, and with the help of her super, the tree was now standing in a corner of the living room.

She was plugging in the lights to make sure they still worked when her intercom buzzed.

"Mrs. Hamilton, you have a guest. Mr. Gerrity is here to see you. Shall I send him up?"

Suzy felt like she had stopped breathing. After a moment, she responded, "Yes."

He had called and texted her several times over the past few days, and she had ignored them all. And now, here he was standing in her doorway.

"I'm sorry to show up unannounced, but I really need to talk to you. Can you just hear me out?"

She motioned for him to come in.

"I was just checking out the Christmas tree lights. Have a seat and I'll get you a glass of wine."

Suzy brought the wine over and sat opposite him.

"Listen, Suzy, I'm so sorry for the way I behaved."

"Well, it's not the first time you've behaved that way. Are you here to tell me you're back with Carol just like you told me thirtysomething years ago that you were going to marry her?" Suzy said, barely able to keep her emotions in check.

"It's not like that at all. And yes, this has to do with Carol, but not in the way you think. Please just let me explain."

With her arms folded, Suzy was in a defensive position waiting to hear the worse. But by the time Devon's story unfolded, all her resolve and defenses had crumbled.

He and Carol had agreed to meet at Mitch Adams's law office on the Tuesday morning after Thanksgiving to sign the papers making Devon the sole owner of Martinique's Vineyard.

Everything went fine with the transfer of ownership, and as soon as the papers were signed, Devon said his goodbyes (and in his mind good riddance) to Carol and left. She went to the ladies' room, but had promised Mitch she'd stop by his office on her way out.

"Carol, come in. I want you to meet my new associate, Ian Hamilton," said Mitch. "Ian is Millie O'Brien's grandnephew. She passed on a few months ago, and left her niece the farmhouse, which is a real bonus for me, because Ian decided to stay out here."

Carol sucked in her breath. "Well then, welcome to the North Fork, Ian. Would your Aunt Millie's niece be Suzy O'Brien by any chance?"

"Yes, that's my mom. Do you know her?"

"Yes, she was one of the summer kids, and as I recall was always following Devon around. And how is your mother?"

"It's been a difficult time since my father died, but coming out here to the North Fork has really helped both of us heal."

"Hmm...I'm sure it has. Well, nice meeting you, Ian. And, Mitch, thank you for all your help."

"My pleasure, Carol. When are you heading back to Paris?"

"In a day or two. I still have some unfinished business."

Later that afternoon she called Devon and asked if she could stop by the beach house early in the evening. "I just thought we should have a little celebratory drink to close everything out on a positive note. Bring one of your bubblies."

That's the last thing I want to do, he thought, but he reluctantly agreed. *A last farewell.*

She showed up at six o'clock, wearing a very low-cut and very short body-hugging dress. He had to admit, she still had a great body.

As he opened the wine, she walked around the beach house, admiring what he'd done with it. And that was when she saw the picture of Suzy and Devon that had been taken over Thanksgiving weekend, arms around each other and looking lovingly into one another's eyes. Suzy hadn't changed much, that bitch. But before saying anything, she laid her trap first.

Devon handed her a glass of wine and invited her to take a seat.

As he went to sit opposite her, she tapped the spot next to her on the sofa. "Devon, don't be silly. Come sit next to me so we can have a proper toast."

He reluctantly sat beside her on the couch.

"Here's to us, Devon. It wasn't all bad, was it?"

They clinked glasses, and Devon agreed there had been some good moments too.

After the first glass, when Devon hadn't offered her another, Carol got up and helped herself.

It was after the second glass that she suddenly wrapped her arms around him, kissed him deeply, and then put her hands in between his legs, whispering in his ear, "You know you want me."

He recoiled. "Carol, enough. You have to leave now."

"Oh, is that because you're back with that little hussy, Suzy? The one who tried to steal you away from me when I went to Paris that summer after college?"

"Carol, what are you talking about? You're the one who left me and told me you didn't want to get married."

"I didn't want to marry you until I found out you were in love with that little white trash girl from the South Shore," she hissed.

"That's enough! I married you, didn't I?""

"Oh yes, dear, you did. But only because I told you I was pregnant."

"I had proposed to you before you were pregnant, in case you forgot."

"Well, here's a news flash...I was *never* pregnant then, and I took birth control pills when we were married when you thought I was trying to get pregnant. I never wanted your child," she hissed.

Devon reeled back in shock to let that sink in.

"You're lying. Of course you were pregnant. I rushed home when you called and told me you miscarried. I held you and we both cried."

"Oh, Devon, you were always so gullible. I was never pregnant. And you got just want you wanted...Daddy's money and the vineyard."

"Damn it, Carol. You know it wasn't like that."

"Oh really? Were you going to marry little miss nobody when Daddy was offering you everything? And let's not forget my daddy took you under his wing from the town drunk who was your father."

"That's enough, Carol. I did love you at one point. And it had nothing to do with your father who I had the utmost respect for, and it was a mutual respect. But now you tell me, after all these years, that you lied about being pregnant and only married me because you were jealous? Get out. Get out of my house now. I'll call a car to take you back to your hotel, but I never, ever want to see your face again."

"I'll ruin you, if it's the last thing I do," Carol raged, her face puckered in hatred as she slammed the door.

Suzy had listened intently as Devon told this tortured story.

"Suzy, I was just so devasted after she told me the truth, with the what-ifs. If she hadn't told me she was pregnant, I would have been with you, and we would have had our child. It was just more than I could handle, and I went into a downward spiral. I love you, Suzy, and I hope you can forgive me."

By then Suzy was in a puddle of tears, and she moved over to the sofa and embraced Devon. "We can't play the what-if game. But we are here now, and I promise to never let you ago again."

CHAPTER 29

THE CARDINAL

Suzy woke up Christmas morning to Elsa leaping on her bed. "Grandma, get up. Santa came." She was so happy that Ian and Elsa had spent Christmas Eve in the apartment and that they were there to open the gifts under her tree. *There is nothing like the delight of a child on Christmas morning.*

She savored every moment of it and then made pancakes before Ian and Elsa headed to Westchester to her other grandparents' home, where Elsa's mom would be waiting for her. They had invited Ian to join them for Christmas dinner. Part of Suzy wished Emily and Ian would get back together, but she knew Ian's heart still belonged to Tatiana. But she was glad they had remained friends for Elsa's sake.

Shortly after they left, Devon arrived as planned to exchange gifts before they headed to dinner at Trish and Michael's home.

Suzy's gift to Devon was perfect. She had taken photos of the beach house, and then commissioned one of Trish's artists to turn it into a magnificent watercolor.

"Suzy...it's just wonderful. The perfect gift," he said as he leaned over and kissed her. "And I have a surprise for you too...and if you don't want it, I'll understand, and you can exchange it for anything you want," he said as he presented her with a box that looked like a hatbox.

Suzy opened it up and removed a beautiful wide-brimmed sun hat, with a bow around the rim. She put it on right away. "I love it. It's perfect for summers on the North Fork."

"There's more. Look under the tissue paper."

And there she found two first-class plane tickets to St. Barts.

"We leave the day after tomorrow and return the day after New Year's. One of my distributors owns a villa on the beach and it's all ours...that is, if you want to go?"

Suzy leaped into his arms. "Oh, Devon, this is perfect. Of course, I want to go."

Soon after, they were making love while Natalie Cole's "This Christmas I Spend with You" played in the background.

~~~~~~

Trish and Michael had prepared a beautiful Christmas dinner—a prime rib with Yorkshire pudding and cheesecake for dessert. During dinner they filled Suzy and Devon in on the community programs they were putting together starting right after the New Year.

"As it turns out, the store next to our gallery came up for rent and we just signed a lease. I'm going to start art classes in the gallery for kids under twelve, and then a program for teenagers. And then next door we'll have programs on healthy living with some of Harlem's health experts, and Michael will start workshops on how to start a business and it will feature
~~~~~~

some of Harlem's successful entrepreneurs. And everything will be free of charge."

"It's great what you two are doing," said Devon. "You know maybe there's a way I can help some of the older teenagers with jobs out East this summer. We can even provide housing."

"That's a terrific idea," said Michael. "Why don't I pour us some single malt scotch and we can grab our coats and sit on the patio, smoke a couple of cigars, and talk about it some more? It's not too cold out today. Do you ladies want to join us?" he said with a wink.

"We'll pass," said Trish. "At least he smokes the cigars outside."

"You and Suzy relax, and I'll clean up the kitchen when we come back in."

"And I'll gladly help," Devon volunteered.

"Perfect," laughed Suzy, "we like our men in aprons."

Trish suggested she and Suzy sit by the fire in their cozy living room, and brought the wine in.

"I'm so happy things worked out with you and Devon. I just knew they would."

"Well, I wasn't so sure, but I'm really happy to get a few days away alone with Devon. We've only had weekends and occasional nights in the city here and there."

They sat contentedly in silence for a few minutes, the way only good friends can. And then Trish sighed.

"What is it?" said Suzy.

"I can't stop thinking about Tatiana. She is getting married on New Year's Day and I think it's such a mistake."

"I know. And Ian never mentions her name, but I know he's still brokenhearted."

Just then, Trish's cell rang. "It's Madge—I'll put her on speaker."

"Well, Merry Christmas from Vermont. How are my two best friends?"

The three of them chatted away. Madge was excited to hear that Devon and Suzy were heading on a romantic getaway. "I've forgotten what those are like," she said laughingly, as she asked the kids if they could quiet down while she talked to Aunt Trish and Aunt Suzy. With that, both kids came to the phone to wish them a Merry Christmas and tell them everything Santa brought them.

When they had finished, Madge said, "You know what? I wouldn't change a thing right now."

After they said their goodbyes to Madge, Suzy turned to Trish.

"You know there's something I've been meaning to tell you. Several times in the past year, a cardinal has appeared in the most unlikely places, and I swear each time the cardinal has peered intently at me and then flown off. I can't help thinking it's some sort of sign. I know this sounds crazy and I'd never mention it to Madge, who would agree it's crazy."

"It's not crazy all. There's a lot of folklore that when a cardinal comes to visit you, it's a visitor from heaven with a message of love for you."

Later that night as Suzy was about to fall asleep with Devon's arm wrapped around her waist, she thought, *It was a wonderful Christmas after all.* And then she dreamed about cardinals.

~~~~~~
~~~~~~

Trish and Michael had a busy week. They wanted to get the new space next to the gallery all set up for their January events. They had posters made up for the windows announcing the various activities. By the time New Year's Eve day came, they were exhausted and decided to spend a quiet evening at home and order dinner in.

It was late in the day and Trish had taken a long relaxing bath and put on her fluffy robe when she heard her phone ringing. She got to it just in time to see Tatiana's name on the screen and quickly answered.

"Tatiana, is something wrong? Isn't your wedding tomorrow?"

"It was. But I canceled it. I'm at JFK Airport and I was hoping if you are home, I might stay there tonight?"

"Oh, my dear, of course you can. Get an Uber and I'll see you soon."

An hour later, an exhausted-looking Tatiana practically fell into Trish's arms at the front door.

Michael grabbed her things and her roller bag and placed them in the guest room while Trish settled her into an oversize chair by the fireplace and brought her a cup of tea.

"I don't want to bombard you with questions," Trish said. "I'm just glad you're here, and you can talk when you feel like it. You look exhausted...you might even want to take a nap in the guest room."

Tatiana smiled gratefully and slept for two hours.

When she awakened, she showered and joined them in time for dinner.

Looking more refreshed, but painfully thin, she said, "I am so glad you were home, and so grateful to both of you for taking me in," she said as she started to tear up. "I didn't know where else to go."

They assured her she was welcome to stay as long she wanted and encouraged her to eat some dinner. Then they told her about their new plans with the gallery and the community events. When they finished dinner, Trish suggested they move into the living room. Feeling more relaxed, that's when Tatiana poured her heart out.

The wedding plans had taken on a life of their own and had consumed her mother's every waking hour as she planned the grandest wedding ever. Tatiana felt no joy in any of it. She could barely eat and had trouble sleeping at night. Nigel, who was always kind and sweet, assured her that it was just all the wedding planning and that once they were married, everything would be wonderful. But deep down Tatiana knew it wouldn't be and that she would be living a lie.

Her mother's younger sister was very concerned and insisted on meeting her for a walk on the beach. "Tatiana, you must look in your heart and ask yourself what it is you really want, not what your mother wants for you."

"I know, but she keeps telling me I must do what is right for the family."

Her aunt looked at her lovingly. "You must do what is right for you. Your mother is a very selfish woman, and she always has been. You belong in New York to pursue your art like your aunt Tania did. It is calling you. And maybe that boy you really love is calling to you too."

"Oh, it's too late for all of that, and I have no money to even get there."

"Here," her aunt said, sliding an envelope from her purse into Tatiana's hand. "There's $10,000 here. It should get you back to New York and tide you over for a bit."

"I can't take this," she protested.

"Oh yes, you can, dear niece. It is part of the money that Tania left to me and I know she is looking down with approval right now."

That afternoon she met with Nigel and told him she couldn't go through with the wedding. He pulled her into his arms and held her for a long time. And then he finally said, "You must follow your dreams," and turned and walked away without looking back.

Then she called the airlines and booked her flight to New York. That night she packed one bag that she tucked under her bed and prepared herself to face her mother the next morning.

"It was even worse than I expected. She said horrible things to me and said I was no longer her daughter and to get out of her house. I spent the night at my aunt's house, and she drove me to the airport. And here I am."

By the time Tatiana finished her story it was almost midnight. Michael left and came back with three glasses of champagne, and as the clock struck twelve, they welcomed in a new year with wishes for only good things to come.

CHAPTER 30

ALL GOOD THINGS RETURN

It was a week after New Year's and the trio had made plans for martinis and dinner to catch up. Madge had a scored a reservation at the hottest new sushi restaurant and they were eager to try the sake martinis.

Trish and Madge immediately wanted to know how the week went with Devon.

"It was wonderful. The villa was stunning, and fully staffed too, so our every little whim was catered to. It was so important for both of us to spend time together away from the vineyards, and to experience just being with each other. It's taken our relationship to a new level." As Suzy talked, she was glowing, and they were so happy for their friend. "And how was Vermont?" she asked Madge.

"It was chaotic wonderfulness. The kids are becoming great little skiers. Jason insisted they learn on regular skies before they could snowboard, but now you can't stop them from snowboarding and Jason loves it too. I can't keep up with any of them. And the best thing is they're exhausted by eight o'clock so Jason and I get some us time, which we've really needed. And by the way, these sake martinis are great."

They sipped their drinks, and then got around to Trish.

"So, tell us about the launch plans for your new community programs," said Madge.

Trish took another sip of her martini. "Yes, Michael and I are really excited, but first, I have some unexpected news to share." She paused while they both just waited.

"Well, tell us!"

"Tatiana is back."

She let it sink in and then told them about the canceled wedding, and her aunt who encouraged her to come back to New York.

"She's staying with us, and Michael and I are delighted. We just adore her. I've also given her space in the gallery to do her painting. And the timing was perfect because I really needed an assistant in the gallery and also someone to teach some of the art classes we have planned. Tatiana was thrilled and at first insisted she didn't want to be paid and would be my assistant in exchange for room and board. We, of course, told her that was a nonstarter, and that I had planned to hire someone. So, there you have it."

"That's great news," said Madge. "It was so sad thinking of her giving up on her dreams."

"Yes, it is wonderful news," Suzy agreed. "What about Ian? Does he know she's back yet? He hasn't said anything to me."

"No. She said she has no right to reach out to him because she treated him so badly. She thinks he must hate her. And I know she is still in love with him, but I couldn't persuade her to contact him. But I told her we were having dinner tonight, and that I was telling you and I was sure you would tell Ian."

"Wow. It's a lot to take in. I'll be on the North Fork this

weekend and I'll try to find the right time to tell Ian. I'm not at all sure how he'll react."

As their sushi rolls and other Japanese delicacies arrived at their table, their talk turned to The Three Tomatoes. Through her sources, Margot had learned that the situation was getting dire. The class action suit had hit the papers, and Margot had some friends in the press who helped to fan the story. Ad sales were still down. The #IWantMyThreeTomatoes was also gaining momentum with the help of some social media experts that she'd hired.

"Margot has already planted a little bug in the ear of North Star's chairman. They were at a holiday cocktail gathering and she mentioned the troubles that were brewing. Then he suggested they have lunch in the New Year. His executive secretary called her the next day and they're having lunch next week."

~~~~~~

Suzy arrived at the beach house Friday afternoon. When she came out for weekends now, she stayed with Devon, but she always made special time to spend with Ian. She had told Devon on one of their late-night calls that Tatiana was back and he agreed that the sooner she told Ian the better. He was bound to find out one way or the other and it was better to hear it from her.

She invited Ian to come to the beach house that night for dinner and joked that it would be okay because Devon was doing the cooking.

He gave his mom a kiss on the cheek when he arrived and presented her with some beautiful flowers too. Devon poured
~~~~~~

him a glass of wine and they sat in the living room with the beautiful high ceilings, and the sounds of the waves lapping the sand. Ian was impressed with her crudité skills. “A little something I learned from Martha Stewart,” she joked.

Ian caught them up on some of the cases he was working on at the law firm, and the latest vineyard updates too.

“Well, if you’ll excuse me, I have a dinner to prepare. We have some fresh Long Island clams and a just-caught flounder,” said Devon.

Suzy took a deep breath and thought, *Here we go.* “Ian, there’s something I have to tell you.”

She was so serious, Ian blurted out, “Mom, you’re not sick, are you?” Ever since he lost his dad, he feared anything happening to his mom.

“No, no, honey. Nothing like that. It’s actually good news, I think...Tatiana is back in New York.”

Ian looked stunned. “Wh-wha-what do you mean, she’s back? She’s back here with her husband?”

“No, Ian. She called off the wedding. She’s staying with Aunt Trish and Uncle Michael and she’s back to painting in Trish’s gallery and also teaching art to some of the local children.”

“How long has she been back?”

“About three weeks.”

“Thanks for letting me know,” he said, getting up. “I’m going to see if Devon needs some help shucking those clams.”

“And that was the end of the conversation,” she told Devon after Ian left.

“Well, give him some time. It must be a shock and he’s going to have to work through it. They both are. If it’s meant to be it will. Look at us,” he said as he took her in his arms.

~~~~~~

Margot Tuttinger had suggested to David's executive assistant that they meet at Michael's. She wanted to be at a place where the press hangs out and were sure to take note of a meeting with her and the chair of North Star, which she knew would happen since she had tipped off a couple of them.

When Margot made her entrance, everyone recognized her. At seventy years old, she could still turn heads and looked like a somewhat older fashion model. She had let her iconic short bob haircut go silver, which flattered her in every way. She was wearing a perfectly tailored winter-white Gucci pantsuit and white Ferragamo booties. Her jewelry was subtle, with simple gold hoop earrings and a gold cuff bracelet.

David rose from his table to kiss her on the cheek. He had obviously arrived early because there was a half-empty martini sitting in front of him.

"Would you like one of these, or would you prefer wine?"

"I'll just have a glass of sparkling water."

They ordered lunch, exchanged pleasantries, and caught up on some gossip of those in their sphere—who was rumored to be getting divorced, etcetera, etcetera. Then there was a little cat and mouse game on who would go first. Margot waited him out.

"You mentioned that you thought The Three Tomatoes was in some trouble, when last we met."

"Well, you know me, David, I don't mince words. Your people bought a great brand and then proceeded to royally fuck it up."

Feigning ignorance, David replied, "Really? I think it's do-
~~~~~~

ing quite well."

"If you call a class action suit, dwindling ad revenues, and formerly loyal subscribers who are mad as hell 'quite well' then I guess you are," Margot retorted.

"And what would you propose, Margot?"

"I propose you sell it back to me and unburden yourself of the embarrassment and the losses too."

"And what would your number be?"

She wrote it on a napkin and handed it to him.

He laughed. "Oh, Margot, you always were a tough negotiator. You know that's an absurd number."

Margot just smiled her catlike smile. "We'll see. Lovely catching up with you, David," she said as she prepared to leave the table.

The next day there were tidbits in the gossip columns that "rumor has it that North Star wants to unload The Three Tomatoes, and Margot Tuttinger just might be the next owner."

Two days later, David's executive assistant called Margot to set up a meeting in his office.

CHAPTER 31
THE COMEBACK

By early March, The Three Tomatoes was reestablished in the loft with Amy at the helm as CEO. Most of the former staff had been rehired too. Thanks to Margot's connections, the doors to the CEOs of several major brands had opened wide for media pitches and she and Suzy were encouraged with the positive response. They had already signed up three leading brands for yearlong media contracts.

Suzy, Madge, and Trish were preparing for a coast-to-coast media blitz later in the month. Amy and her team were also putting together two summits for June in New York City and Los Angeles with a terrific lineup of speakers with topics ranging from health and wellness, to upping your style game, travel, and more. The trio would be there as well to celebrate the rebirth of The Three Tomatoes with their loyal subscribers.

"Sometimes you get what you wish for," said Madge laughingly, as they gathered for their martini meetup before their Ripe Tomatoes dinner.

"Yes, it's going to be a crazy month with the media tour,

but I'm looking forward to seeing our friends tonight," added Suzy.

"I still can't quite believe how Margot pulled this off, but I couldn't be happier to have our baby back," Trish chimed in as they toasted each other.

Dinner with the Ripe Tomatoes was a joyous occasion celebrating The Three Tomatoes comeback. Everyone had made an effort to be there, and Hope made a lovely toast.

"To three of the most special women I know—here's to all the successes you so richly deserve."

The conversation then turned to the Tony nominations. Voting was taking place now and the nominees would be announced in April. Hope and Ellen were anxiously awaiting the results.

"This is a very big budget production and while short-term sales are great, winning a Tony or even being nominated always helps with future sales," said Hope.

"And it will help with investors for our new projects," added Ellen, "which is going a little slower than we hoped right now."

Arlene had big news too. "Bill and I have decided to move in together."

They were all happy for her and also glad to hear she was being cautious too. "Believe it or not, Bill always rented in New York, so he's giving up his apartment and we're going to find another rental to move into together. But I'm keeping my apartment and since I'm in a condo, I'll be able to rent it."

Suzy was glad to hear this because she wasn't at all sure that Bill's roving eye had stopped roving, a thought she would never share with Arlene, but she was glad to hear she had a plan B.

When the conversation turned to Heather, Hope, never shy, asked her how her love life was going, expecting Heather's usual answer that with her demanding career she didn't have time to date.

So, they were all surprised when she responded, "Well, I've been seeing someone for a couple of months now." But even though they all prodded her for more information, she just smiled.

Madge made a mental note to call Heather and have lunch soon so she could get the real story.

Celeste had been uncharacteristically quiet all evening, and Suzy thought she looked a little pale. They were seated next to each other, and as they were all getting up to leave, Suzy noticed Celeste was a little unstable on her feet. Without drawing attention, Suzy wrapped her arm in Celeste's and walked her out the door.

"Celeste, are you okay?" she asked, concerned when they reached the sidewalk.

"Oh, I'm fine, dear. Just a little tired."

"Well, let me take you home."

"No need for that, I'm fine, really. And here's my car now."

Suzy hoped that was true.

~~~~~~

When Madge was heading back to Brooklyn, she texted Heather. "Hey, free for lunch this week? I want to hear about the new love." They picked a Midtown lunch spot near Heather's broadcast studio the following day.

"Are you up for all the media hoopla?" Heather asked.

"It's so different being on the other side," Madge said.
~~~~~~

"First, dealing with the media during Jason's campaign and now with our media tour. I think the press side is less stressful," she laughed.

"Well, I'm excited to do a segment with the three of you for our evening magazine show, and I'm hoping the media everywhere picks up on the message that women in midlife and beyond have powerful voices that need to be heard."

"Here's hoping," said Madge as they dug into their salads.

After a few forkfuls, Heather said, "You're being very patient, Madge, and I know you're dying to ask me what's up with the new person in my life."

"Whatever are you talking about? But yes, spill the beans."

"It happened quite unexpectedly and took me by surprise, but I'm finally in love for the first time."

"That's wonderful news. Who is he?"

And then Heather dropped the bombshell. "It's not a *he*, it's a *she*."

Without any hesitation, Madge put her hand over Heather's and said, "He or she or they, I'm just so happy for you. Tell me all about her."

"Oh, Madge, thank you. It's such a relief to tell someone. Anna is her name. She's beautiful, smart, openly gay, and heads up a major nonprofit. I never thought I'd be in love with a woman, yet here I am head over heels and I'm not quite sure what to do about it."

Heather had never thought of herself as gay. Over the years she had dated a string of eligible men, but after she had been sexually harassed and assaulted by her former boss, who had done the same thing to Madge years before, she froze when any man tried to get intimate with her.

"And then I interviewed Anna for a segment on our news

magazine, and the next day she invited me for drinks. Before I knew it, we were in an intimate relationship unlike any I have ever known before. But I'm so conflicted, Madge. Not about her, but about coming out with this publicly and how it might affect my career."

"I'd like to think that, in this day and age, that won't happen. But the reality is the tabloids will have a field day."

"I know, Madge, that's what I'm worried about. And I don't want Anna dragged through all that, although she's getting impatient for us to go public."

"I think there's never going to be a good time, but I know you'll figure out the right time. And Jason and I would love to meet her. Let's pick a night for dinner after our media tour is over."

"Thanks, Madge. You're a great friend."

"So are you."

And they truly were. Madge could never have imagined a few years back when they considered themselves rivals that they would ever become dear friends. Shared trauma and time changes everything.

CHAPTER 32
IAN AND TATIANA

After two exhausting, but exhilarating weeks on a national media tour, they were finally heading home. "Thank goodness for Jason's private plane," said Trish. "It made this trip so much easier, and the three of us haven't spent this much time together since we were roommates."

"That's true, although staying in five-star suites that were about three times the size of our little apartment was definitely an upgrade," laughed Suzy.

"You know, as glad as I am to be going home to see Jason and the kids, I'm going to miss our special time together too," said Madge as they toasted each other with champagne.

A car was waiting for them at Teterboro. They dropped Trish off first, and then Suzy. They said their goodbyes and Madge headed home to Brooklyn.

Devon was already at Suzy's apartment and she dropped her bags in the hall and embraced him at the door. "God, I've missed you," he said as he inhaled her hair. "Let's get your things inside and I'll pour us some wine."

Suzy changed into more comfortable clothes, kicked off

her shoes, and plopped on the couch next to Devon.

"It was a great couple of weeks, but I am so glad to be home."

"I knew you'd be tired, so I took the liberty of ordering in from our favorite little Italian restaurant."

"Another reason I love you, Mr. Gerrity, you're always one step ahead."

Over dinner Suzy told him all about the tour and how excited they were for all the great press. Devon caught her up on the latest news from the North Fork, including a couple of nice dinners he had enjoyed with Ian.

"Has he mentioned Tatiana at all?"

"Not a word. But we did talk about your vineyard and some of his ideas for the future. He has such a great business mind. And he gave me a heads-up on a vineyard I'd like to buy."

"You're buying another vineyard?"

"I'm hoping to. It all came up quickly. We've been there. It's The Old Barn that has that beautiful tasting room in a restored old barn. And they produce a very nice chardonnay."

"Yes, I love that place."

"The owner died before Christmas and everyone thought the kids would take over, but they're not interested. They approached Mitch Adams who is handling their dad's estate about finding a buyer quickly, and Ian thought I might be interested. So, I've made them a very fair market value offer, which I hope they'll accept."

"Oh, that's wonderful. I'm surprised though because I know you never wanted to get too big."

"Well, it's small enough that we can operate it separately, and I'd rather buy it than have some soulless corporation gobble up another one of our small vineyards."

"That's very exciting," Suzy said, but she couldn't help stifling a yawn.

"And now I think it's time we get you into bed, or rather in bed." Devon smiled at a very sleepy Suzy. "There's always the morning," he said as he kissed the top of her head.

~~~~~~

It was a chilly early April day, but one that's always welcome after winter. Trish and Tatiana had gone jogging together in Central Park and had stopped to admire the daffodils and hyacinths that were jutting up everywhere, before returning home to get ready to head to the gallery.

Trish and Michael were so happy to have Tatiana back and they had encouraged her to continue to stay with them. She was the daughter they had always wanted. Tatiana's new work was brilliant, and Trish was looking forward to exhibiting it in a few weeks.

They arrived at the gallery for the Saturday art classes they offered to the community. The morning classes were for the younger children, and Trish especially loved how wonderful and patient Tatiana was teaching them. They set up the easels and the paints, and Trish headed into the office to catch up on some of the gallery work she was behind on since the media tour.

It was almost noon when she walked back into the gallery just in time to see Ian coming in. Tatiana was in the back room cleaning up paintbrushes.

"Hi, Aunt Trish," he said as he hugged her.

"Ian, what a surprise. What brings you into the city today?"
~~~~~~

"I had a little business to attend to and then I thought I'd drop by and see Tatiana. Is she here?"

Just then Tatiana appeared in her paint-covered smock and stopped short.

"Oh my God, Ian...wha-wha-what are you doing here?"

"I was hoping I could steal you away for lunch, if that's okay with you, Aunt Trish?"

She tried to play it cool and contain her joy. "Of course, Ian," she said hoping it didn't sound like she had put an exclamation point at the end of that.

And so it began, slowly at first, that Ian and Tatiana found their way back together.

~~~~~~

It was a beautiful weekend in late April. Suzy and Tatiana were sitting on the front porch of the farmhouse enjoying a glass of wine while Ian and Devon were shucking oysters and firing up the grill. It was Tatiana's first visit to the farmhouse.

"In my country, it would be the men sitting on the porch and the women in the kitchen."

"Well, fortunately for everyone, the men in my life are good cooks, but I am very good at making reservations."

Tatiana laughed her lyrical laugh that was so like her Aunt Tania's.

"So, what do you think of the North Fork so far?"

"Oh, it is so beautiful and peaceful. It's hard to believe that just a couple of hours away from the hustle and bustle and noise of Manhattan that we could be sitting in such a magical place. Now I know why Ian loves it here. I've had my sketch pad everywhere and I am inspired to paint everything I see
~~~~~~

here."

"Perhaps that will be your next exhibit. Trish is so excited about the latest paintings. And I just want to say, I am so very happy that you made the decision to return to New York. You're already having an impact on the art scene here, not to mention the impact you have by making my son happy."

Tatiana smiled that beautiful smile of hers. "He makes me very happy too."

"Let's join the guys in the kitchen. We can drink wine and watch them cook."

As they walked in, Devon was saying to Ian that he still didn't understand how he had lost the bid to buy The Old Barn vineyard. He had been so disappointed when he called Suzy earlier in the week and told her he lost the bid.

"It was a shock to Mitch and me too," said Ian. "The sale was really kept quietly under the radar, and we still don't know who this company really is. They sent in lawyers with proxies at the closing. We cautioned the family about selling, but it was an offer they would have had a very hard time turning down."

"Well, it's very strange. It's not a bid I was willing to outmatch, since I was offering the fair market value, but it's almost as if someone didn't want me to have it."

"I guess we'll know in due time who the owner is," said Ian.

CHAPTER 33

MYSTERIES AND COMING OUT

"It's like old times," Trish said as she looked around the conference table at the loft offices of The Three Tomatoes. Madge and Suzy smiled in agreement. It was the first official staff meeting they had all been to since the reboot. Margot had joined them too.

When Amy told the staff that Ms. Tuttinger would be there, they were all a little nervous to be presenting to her since her "The Devil Wears Prada" reputation had preceded her. Margot put everyone at ease at the very beginning of the meeting by asking them to please call her Margot. Then she said how pleased she was with how quickly they had reenergized the brand and that they were exceeding her expectations. Then she added, "I'm only here to listen." There was a collective sigh of relief.

The room was charged with energy and there was a lot to be excited about. Their subscriber numbers now exceeded their previous high. More brands were coming on board as advertisers. And the coast-to-coast June summits were already sold out.

"We had to get larger rooms for the opening night cocktail reception where attendees who bought VIP tickets can personally meet Suzy, Trish, and Madge in both L.A. and New York," reported their event manager. "They all want to meet you."

They spent some time talking about the event. The speaker roster included the female CEO of one of the biggest corporations in America, a beloved multiple Oscar-winning actress who was redefining ageism in America, and several panels of top experts in health and wellness. The closing panel would be Suzy, Madge, and Trish and would be moderated by Heather, just as their very first summit was more than five years ago.

"And, Madge, do you think you'll have a trailer for the documentary?" Amy asked.

"Actually, I have a sneak peek to show you all right now."

Madge had started working on her latest documentary *The Haves and the Have-Nots* shortly after the election. The focus was on the disparity in disadvantaged populations in everything from health care to education to life spans.

"We're hoping to complete final edits over the summer and premiere it in New York this fall. So, June is the perfect time to start promoting it. Here you go," she said as she clicked the remote to start the video.

The three-minute trailer ended and there was a moment of silence while Madge held her breath. And then everyone in the room applauded.

"That was a powerful three minutes," said Amy.

Then Margot spoke up. "I know I said I'd be quiet, but Madge, I think you have another award-winning documentary in the works."

After the meeting ended, Suzy, Trish, Madge, and Margot

headed up to the loft apartment for lunch. Amy begged off because she had summit details she was working on. Before they headed up, Margot made a point to tell Amy what a terrific job she and her staff were doing.

It was a beautiful day, and they brought their lunch out onto the terrace. They continued discussing business for a while and then the conversation turned to Keri's upcoming nuptials over Memorial Day weekend.

"Has she turned into bridezilla yet?" Madge said laughingly.

"She's been surprisingly calm," said Suzy. "And especially since what started out as a very small intimate wedding has grown to one hundred and fifty. Thank goodness the wedding planner at Devon's vineyard is such a pro, and that they could accommodate the last-minute changes."

"Well, Bitania has been practicing throwing rose petals on the ground for weeks now by spewing potpourri all over the house."

Trish added how honored Michael was when Keri called him and asked if he would walk her down the aisle. Suzy smiled, and silently wiped away a little tear.

Margot, who was not known for her "girlfriend" chitchat skills, saw that as her cue to leave.

Suzy started to thank her for the umpteenth time for saving The Three Tomatoes. With a wave of her hand, she interrupted Suzy. "It was you who have saved me from a frivolous and indulgent retirement. It's great to be back in the thick of things." And with that she was gone.

"Well, I think we all have to get going," said Madge. "We have the gala this evening for Anna's nonprofit and I need to check in with Heather to see how her nerves are. It will be the first time she and Anna will be appearing together in public as a couple. See you both later."

~~~~~~

Devon was in town for the gala and for some meetings with a couple of his distributors. He arrived back at Suzy's apartment late in the afternoon. "Let's relax on the terrace. We have time before we have to get ready for the evening."

They sat quietly for a few minutes and Suzy sensed Devon was stressed. "How were your meetings?"

"Not good. My distributor who sells our wines to the top restaurants in the city is cutting his orders back by 50 percent. Seems The Old Barn has cut a deal with him to buy their chardonnays at a ridiculously low price. I don't get it. They have to be losing money."

"Devon, that's awful. What do you think is going on?"

"It's very strange. We still don't know who really owns The Old Barn, but it's almost as if someone has it in for me."

~~~~~~

The cocktail reception was the typical overcrowded noisy scene filled with air-kisses and people who pretended to have conversations while they looked around the room to see if there was someone more notable they should be seen with.

Now that Jason was a senator, there was a nonstop pilgrimage to have a word with him while hoping the photographer would catch a shot. "Christ," he whispered to Madge, "I can't even finish a glass of wine."

"That's what happens when you become powerful. I hate

to leave your side, but I need to check in with Heather."

Heather had made her way over to where Suzy and Trish were standing, and Madge joined them.

"You look stunning," Madge said to her. She was dressed is a simple but elegant vintage designer gown in navy, accessorized with only a delicate gold chain, a gift from Anna.

"Wish I was sitting at the table with all of you, but Anna insisted I be at the head table. And she wants me by her side for the photos during the after-reception. This is really happening," she said nervously.

They soon headed into the ballroom that accommodated a thousand people, and there wasn't an empty seat. The dinners were eventually served, either overcooked or cold by the time they arrived at the tables, but fortunately the wineglasses were always kept full, and attendees chatted away at their tables completely ignoring the speeches. And like most galas of this nature, it ran too long, and the generous applause at the end was really in thanks that the evening was finally ending, and they could head back out to the reception area for more schmoozing, desserts, and after-dinner drinks.

Heather had joined the trio when Anna spotted her and made her way over. Anna looked beautiful as well this evening in an elegant yet sexy tuxedo suit. She slipped her arm comfortably around Heather's waist and thanked them all for their support.

"And now I need to steal Heather away for some photos." She smiled with her arm still firmly around Heather's waist. There was no mistaking they were a couple.

The next morning Madge immediately went to Page Six, and front and center was a beautiful photo of Anna and Heather, with a caption that said, Broadcast journalist Heather Stone confirms she's in a relationship with the CEO of one of the country's leading nonprofits.

Madge texted Heather. "Congratulations. You look beautiful and happy together."

CHAPTER 34
THE BEST LAID PLANS

"It's going to be perfect weather for the wedding," Trish said as they were in the car heading out to the North Fork. Michael was behind the wheel and Tatiana was in the back seat.

"I think you'll like the beautiful Victorian inn we're staying at on Shelter Island. It has a huge porch where you can watch the sunset," Trish said to Tatiana. "We take a short little ferry ride to get there, and you can walk or bike around the island. And it's where the rehearsal dinner is tonight."

Ian had wanted Tatiana to stay at the farmhouse, but his daughter was coming, and she told Ian it would not be proper to sleep in his room while she was there. Plus, they needed space for his family members at the house too. Ian had grinned and said, "Well, I'll just have to sneak over to Shelter Island."

The farmhouse was a flurry of activity. Madge and Jason had arrived earlier in the day with the kids, and Elsa and Bitania were totally wired with the excitement of being in the wedding party. Madge was going to spend the night at the farmhouse with Bitania to help get the girls dressed the next day so Suzy could focus on Keri.

Keri threw her arms around Madge when she arrived. She and her very cool Aunt Madge had always had a special relationship and there were things she could tell her that she never told her mother.

Madge held her tightly, and then whispered, “If you have any doubts at all just say the word, and I’ll help you escape.”

Keri gave her a tight hug back. “I know you would. I’m nervous, not about being married to Chris, but about this big wedding now. I’m wishing we had eloped.”

Madge laughed. “Well, that would have saved your mom a lot of money, but I know how excited she is to see you walk down the aisle.”

The wedding rehearsal was scheduled for five o’clock at the vineyard and then they’d head to Shelter Island for the rehearsal dinner.

Devon was waiting to greet them all and led them outside to the area where the ceremony would take place. The weather forecast looked good, but the fallback was to have the ceremony inside the tasting room. The reception would still be in the huge tent they had rented.

Everything looked perfect. The wedding planner gathered them all to the area where the ceremony would take place. The wedding would be officiated by Chris’s uncle who was an ordained minister. Suzy wasn’t particularly religious, but she was glad it was a real minister and not a friend who signed up on the internet to be a wedding officiant the day before, as was so often the case these days.

The rehearsal went smoothly. Yonas took his role as ring bearer very seriously and was nervous he’d drop the ring, which Jason assured him would not happen. And the girls were so excited Suzy wondered if they'd ever get them to sleep tonight. Chris had asked Ian to be his best man, a testament to how close they had become. And Keri had asked her best friend and college roommate to be her maid of honor. That was the wedding party.

Devon had hired a large boat to take them all to the restaurant on Shelter Island. It was a beautiful evening and Suzy was overwhelmed with so many emotions, but mostly she was just grateful to be alive for the biggest moment, so far, in her daughter's life. She sent a little prayer up to Ken, but she felt that somehow he was with them too. The dinner had been lovely and Suzy and Chris's dad both made touching speeches welcoming the couple into their families.

When they got back to the dock in Greenport, she hugged Devon and kissed him good-night. "I'll see you at the vineyard tomorrow. Thanks for everything you've done to make this wedding wonderful."

~~~~~~

It was three o'clock in the morning when the fire chief called Devon. There was a fire at the vineyard. He threw on some clothes and drove as fast as he could.

He could smell the acrid smoke and saw the flames shooting up into the night sky. They had barricades everywhere and a cop tried to stop him from going farther when the fire chief spotted him.

"How bad is it?"

"The wedding tent in the back is destroyed, but we've got the fire contained so it can't reach the vines. But the tasting room and the offices went up like a tinderbox. I can't get any
~~~~~~

of my guys in there until it's out and safe to go in."

"Well, thank God it happened in the middle of night and no one's here. But I don't understand how the fire could have started."

"Listen, Devon, this isn't official because we won't know for a while, but there are signs it could be arson."

"Arson? Who would want to do that?" Devon put his face in his hands. "And the wedding tomorrow is for Suzy's daughter. I dread telling her this."

Devon went home distraught and paced around the beach house. He was still trying to wrap his head around the idea that it could be arson. And equally upsetting was that the fire had also destroyed Keri's wedding. Then he had an idea. *It just might work.*

~~~~~~

He had been up the rest of night putting his plan together, but waited until eight o'clock to head to the farmhouse to tell Suzy. The children and Keri were still asleep, but Suzy, Madge, and Ian were drinking coffee on the porch when he pulled up.

"Devon, what a nice surprise, but what are you doing here so early?"

He then broke the news to the three of them.

Suzy started to cry.

"Wait, I have an idea that can save the wedding. We can do it here, right out in back of the farmhouse."

"But, Devon, nothing is landscaped in the back. Ian is still working on the plans for exactly where to plant the vines and he's waiting to start that before finishing the landscaping."

"I've been on the phone with Annie, our wedding planner,
~~~~~~

since early this morning and she's on the case. We've called in some favors, and we can have a tent set up by noon, and the area for the ceremony too. We'll set up another tent for the caterers and have everything delivered here. Annie has talked to one of the local nurseries and they'll bring in some container trees and beautiful flowers. Since the ceremony doesn't start until five o'clock we should be good to go."

"Devon, do you really think you can make all that happen in time for the ceremony?"

"We'll move heaven and earth."

"Let me know what I can do," said Ian.

"And Trish and I can make sure we get ahold of all the wedding guests, so they know there's a change of venues," said Madge.

"I hope we can pull this off," said Suzy. "Now I just have to tell the bride-to-be that we're still 'going to the chapel and she's gonna get married' but we've moved the chapel."

~~~~~~

Somehow it all came together, and before the guests arrived the back area of the farmhouse had been transformed into a magical outdoor paradise. And what a story Keri and Chris would have to tell their children one day.

Suzy wore a mint-colored silk midi-sheath from her designer friend, Gabrielle Carlson, and looked beautiful as she was escorted down the aisle by Ian to her seat. She smiled at all the wonderful friends who were here today. Of course, there were Trish and Michael, and Jason and Madge, and with the exception of Celeste who was in London, all the Ripe Tomatoes were there. *We've all shared so much together*, she
~~~~~~

thought—the good times and the bad times, and it was wonderful to share this special happy time together.

Everyone smiled when Elsa and Bitania skipped down the aisle gleefully throwing rose petals on the white runner. And when everyone stood and turned to see Michael walk Keri down the aisle, there was an audible gasp. She looked so beautiful and so happy, there was not a dry eye.

Sometime after the dinner had been served buffet style, the dancing started. They had hired a great local band that had just about everyone up dancing. Suzy had been so busy greeting everyone she hadn't hit the dance floor yet. She felt a gentle tap on her shoulder, "May I have this dance?"

Devon held her closely as the singer sang, "You Are So Beautiful" and Devon quietly sang the lyrics in her ear.

"Devon, I love you so much. You turned a horrible tragedy for you into a perfect wedding for Keri and I'm sure you're still in shock about the vineyard."

"Suzy, tonight is for lovers. As Scarlett O'Hara once said, 'Tomorrow is another day.'"

When tomorrow came, there was more news about the vineyard. Shocking news.

CHAPTER 35
REVENGE

Suzy had planned to head back to the city on Monday, which was Memorial Day, but she and Devon were still reeling from the news he had received from the fire chief on Sunday, and she stayed on with him at the beach house.

Suzy had hosted a brunch on Sunday at the farm for close family and friends, when she noticed Devon had quietly disappeared. He returned a short time later and looked ashen.

"Devon, what's happened?"

"I'll tell you after everyone leaves."

For the next couple of hours Suzy played the gracious host, and then they all hugged and kissed Keri and Chris goodbye. Ian had volunteered to drive them to the airport for their flight to Maui and Tatiana was going along for the ride. He had quietly asked his mother earlier if they could stay in the apartment that night.

Madge, Jason, and the kids were the last to leave. Elsa was excitedly going with them and spending the night since Monday was a holiday. Ian would pick her up Monday and take her home to her mom.

"Devon, let's sit. Tell me what's happened."

"They found a body in the ashes of the tasting room."

"On my God! Do they know who it is?"

"They know it's a woman, but the body is so badly charred right now they're going to need more information to identify her. And they think the fire is suspicious and that, whoever this person is, she could be the arsonist."

Suzy took Devon in her arms.

"I'm so sorry, Suzy."

"What do you have to be sorry for?"

"This was such a special time for you with Keri and now this has put a damper on everything."

"Devon, it was still special. And now I'm just worried about you." Suzy had a premonition that the worst wasn't over yet.

~~~~~~

Two days later, the fire chief and the police chief showed up at the beach house. Devon had known them both since childhood.

"Devon, we found something in the ashes, and we think it will identify the body."

Confused, he invited them in. "Do you remember Suzy O'Brien, Millie O'Brien's niece?"

"Oh sure," they both said as they shook hands with Suzy.

"Please sit," Devon said.

"Listen, sorry to barge in like this, but we found a gold wedding ring in the ashes, and we think you might be able to identify it."

With that they handed Devon a plastic bag that contained a gold wedding ring.
~~~~~~

The police chief continued, “The lettering inside reads *DG to CH* with a date.”

Stunned, Devon looked at the inside of the ring through the plastic.

“Oh my God. That’s Carol’s wedding ring. How would that be in the ashes from the fire?”

“Because we think the charred body is Carol’s.”

“That’s impossible. Carol went back to France months ago, right after I bought out her share of the vineyard.”

“We’re checking into all of that, Devon. We’re having her dental records pulled to confirm if she is the deceased. And if she is, it’s likely she is the one who set the fire. We should know more in a few days.”

Suzy put her arm around Devon’s shoulder. He was clearly in shock.

“We’re sorry, Devon,” said the fire chief. “Good to see you again, Suzy. Wish it was under better circumstances.”

When they left, Devon said, “Let’s take a walk on the beach. I need to clear my head.”

~~~~~~

By the end of the week the sordid story was revealed. The body was confirmed as Carol’s. She had come back from Paris twice since her last encounter with Devon when she had promised “she would ruin him.” Each time she stayed at a B&B on Shelter Island. As the picture started to come into view for Devon, he suspected that she was the one who bought The Old Barn vineyard. After inquiries into the ownership of The Old Barn, the police discovered it had been purchased by an LLC called Revenge. Further digging led to a New York City law
~~~~~~

firm that confirmed that Revenge LLC was owned by Carol. Among her things in the B&B was the local newspaper clipping announcing the wedding plans of the grandniece of the late Millie O'Brien.

They suspected she had started the fatal fire, and it had gotten out of control before she could get out of the tasting room. But they didn't have concrete evidence.

Devon and Suzy were in disbelief.

"She didn't want me, but she didn't want you to have me either," Devon said shaking his head.

"Listen, Devon. She was obviously a very disturbed woman. There was no way you could have seen this coming. Believe me, I saw Trish and Michael go through dealing with a psychotic woman, and Michael spent way too much time blaming himself. You have to let this go."

"Well, there is one thing I have to do. This is a small town, and none of us need this kind of scandal. Carol's father was a good man, and I don't want this to become part of his legacy." He called Mitch Adams.

The story that was released to the press contained few details. It stated that the body of Carol Hopkins, the daughter of John Hopkins and one of the North Fork's most prominent families, had been found in the fire at Martinique's Vineyard, that was ruled accidental. There was no speculation as to why she was at the tasting room in the middle of the night. However, there were unconfirmed reports that she had been at one of the local taverns who refused to serve her anymore. And she had left, saying "I know where to get more." A sad and tragic ending to the life of a woman few on the North Fork had ever even liked.

A few days later, Devon and Mitch Adams were the only

two at the graveside where they buried Carol's remains next to her father's.

Mitch had asked Devon to come to his offices after the burial for the reading of Carol's will. Mitch told Devon that after the divorce he had suggested to Carol on a few occasions that she might want to update her will.

"She always blew me off, and so her last will and testament is still in good standing. She has left her entire estate to you, Devon."

He went on to detail the assets. There was the apartment in Paris, and a few hundred thousand dollars left in the trust her father had set up for her. It had been substantially more when he died, but Carol liked to live big.

"And Devon, she took the money from the buyout of Martinique's and used that to buy The Old Barn, and you are now the owner."

CHAPTER 36

THE REBOOT AND A SAD FAREWELL

The day of The Three Tomatoes's Reboot Yourself Summit in New York City had arrived. Trish, Suzy, and Madge were in the speakers' room that had monitors where they could watch the event. They were still on a glorious natural high from the VIP reception the night before. Over five hundred women had paid $1,000 to attend and personally meet them, and a portion of the proceeds were going to a wonderful organization that focused on educating girls in disadvantaged communities.

They had made an effort to walk the room and personally shake the hands of as many women as they could, and each woman they talked to thanked them for bringing back "their" Three Tomatoes.

The event was going really well and the buzz among the attendees during lunch was all positive. Their luncheon keynote speaker was the Oscar-winning actress everyone adored. She talked about fighting ageism in Hollywood and being a spokeswoman only for brands that didn't airbrush every wrinkle from her face or want her to color her silver locks. And then she did the lead up to the trailer for Madge's upcoming documentary, *The Haves and the Have-Nots*. When the trailer finished, everyone in the room was on their feet applauding.

Suzy and Trish looked at Madge and gave her a thumbs-up.

They were the last speakers and usually by the end of a long day of speakers and panels the audience would thin out. But not today.

Heather walked onto the stage to enthusiastic applause. "Five years ago, I had the honor of introducing three incredible women who had founded a little media company that celebrates women at every age and every stage. And today I couldn't be more honored to introduce them again..."

After they were seated, Heather got a huge laugh from the audience when she said, "So, ladies, anything interesting happen in the past year?"

They talked about the growth of The Three Tomatoes, the offer they couldn't refuse, and then their disappointment in the direction after the buyout. But it was Suzy who summed it up beautifully at the end of their discussion.

"The reason we are back, stronger than ever, is all because each and every one of you and all the other women across the country were fed up with being invisible, marginalized, and not having your voices heard. You stood up to ageism by your protests at the headquarters of one of the giants in entertainment. You took to social media with the hashtag, #IWantMyThreeTomatoes, and you never gave up. We heard you. You gave us the courage to reboot."

As she was talking, ushers were walking up and down each

aisle handing out mini megaphones to all the attendees.

"And now grab your megaphones and let's shout out to the world, 'Can you hear us now?'"

The audience went wild with the thunderous roar of fifteen hundred women chanting, "Can you hear us now?"

As they walked off the stage, Madge turned to Trish and Suzy and in her signature line, said, "It's so fucking hot in here," and this time she wasn't talking about hot flashes, but the excitement of the audience.

The following week in L.A., they experienced the same excitement and enthusiasm from attendees. They were back, better than ever.

~~~~~~

The Sunday after they returned from L.A. was the Tony Awards. Madge had invited Trish, Michael, Suzy, and Devon for dinner and to watch the televised awards show.

Jason made a beautiful toast to "the unstoppable" trio at dinner. "You are the most extraordinary women I have ever known. You're smart, beautiful, generous, loyal, and honestly more adjectives than I even know. You're making the world a better place, and I think I can speak for Michael and Devon, you each make us better men." Devon and Michael raised their glasses in agreement.

After dinner, Madge suggested they have their desserts in the den so they wouldn't miss the start of the awards ceremony.

When they got to the announcement for the Best Musical, they were all on the edge of their seats. As soon as they announced the winner, Suzy, Trish, and Madge were leaping
~~~~~~

around the room with joy. "They did it!"

They squeezed each other's hands when Hope came to the microphone, each thinking, *Please don't be unfiltered, Hope.* And to everyone's relief, she gave a heartfelt acceptance speech and acknowledged the rocky start, "...but one that ended with a fabulous musical and cast and this honor. However, the best part is yet to come, and I hope there will be many more wonderful shows with the best producing partner ever," and then she brought Ellen to the podium.

~~~~~~

The next morning Suzy's phone buzzed, and Hope's name popped up on the screen. Suzy was looking forward to hearing all the highlights of the evening.

"Hope, I can't wait to hear...."

But before she could finish her sentence, Hope said, "Suzy, I have sad news. I just heard from Sir Oliver. Celeste passed away last night."

By late afternoon, Hope had all the details and shared them with the Ripe Tomatoes, who were all devasted by this loss.

Sir Oliver told Hope that Celeste's heart was failing for quite a while. She did not want any extraordinary measures taken and she didn't want anyone to know her health was faltering.

"Her desire was to spend her final days in our rose garden with me by her side, and to die on her own terms. That's what we did. She passed away peacefully in her sleep," he said.

He told Hope that Celeste wanted a small private funeral in England and to be cremated with some of her remains
~~~~~~

placed in Sir Oliver's family cemetery on the grounds of his estate. But she had agreed to a memorial service in New York City and requested that Hope plan it.

~~~~~~

Three weeks later, Hope had emailed the Ripe Tomatoes with a date for their first dinner since Celeste's death. But it came with an intriguing request.

"The day before our dinner, I need you all to meet me at the Helen Hayes Theater at noon."

So, on a very warm July day, all the Ripe Tomatoes showed up at the theater. It was a Monday, so there were no shows there.

Hope greeted them in the lobby. "This is the theater we opened our show, *If Tomorrow Never Comes,* that eventually moved to Broadway and won Celeste a Tony for Best Playwright and won me my first Tony for Best Musical. So, I thought it was only fitting that we meet here so that I can give each of you your assignments before our dinner tomorrow night."

They all looked at her, puzzled.

"When I met with Sir Oliver last week to talk about the memorial, he gave me a plastic bag filled with some of Celeste's ashes. It was her desire that I give each of the Ripe Tomatoes a few of her ashes and that each of us sprinkle them in some of her favorite spots around the city. I've already started by placing a few ashes under a floorboard of the stage here."

With that Hope presented each of them with a small bag of ashes, and an envelope with the designated spot where they should place them. They were stunned.
~~~~~~

"And tomorrow night I've arranged for a private room at our usual place for dinner and we will share where we have placed the ashes of our beautiful friend."

They all dispersed, but not before Trish suggested to Suzy and Madge that they join her at the Starbucks next door.

"Okay, let's all see what we've got," said Madge.

They had the New York Public Library, MoMA, and Celeste's favorite department store, Saks Fifth Avenue.

"Let's do this together," suggested Suzy, "although I'm not even sure this is legal." But off they went.

The New York Public Library on Fifth Avenue was a no-brainer. There was a grassy area with flowers and shrubs on each side of the famous lions, Patience and Fortitude. Trish and Suzy stood guard, while Madge quickly stepped over the low trellis and sprinkled ashes around the azaleas. They said a quick little prayer, but couldn't help laughing at their antics. MoMA was next.

"I know," said Trish. "We can sprinkle a few ashes in the reflecting pool in the sculpture garden."

They sat on one of the benches by the pool while Trish casually strolled closer to the pool and sprinkled in a few ashes. Again, they said a little prayer, and then couldn't stop laughing at their cloak-and-dagger adventure.

Saks Fifth Avenue proved a little more challenging.

"Well, we can't just sprinkle ashes anywhere in the store," Suzy said discouraged, after they had been roaming around for half an hour.

"Wait...I have an idea," said Madge. "When we came in there were window designers creating the displays for fall. Here's my idea."

"Let's hope this works," said Trish.

Madge approached one of the window designers who was standing on a ladder. "Excuse me, we're just curious what the fall display will look like."

He appeared quite annoyed to be interrupted, until he recognized Madge. "Oh my gosh, you're Madge Thompson!"

And while Madge chatted him up, Suzy sprinkled a few ashes in one of the wells that housed a floodlight in one of the main windows facing Fifth Avenue that was directly across the street from Rockefeller Plaza.

When they got outside, they were laughing so hard they were practically peeing in their pants.

That was when they realized that Celeste had so cleverly planned the placement of her ashes, just as she would do in one of her best-selling novels, to make sure that they sent her off with joy and laughter instead of tears and sadness.

~~~~~~

The next night they sat in the private room upstairs and each shared their stories of scattering Celeste's ashes. Each story was funnier than the next.

"I had to pay an usher to place a tiny bag of ashes in the orchestra pit of the Metropolitan Opera House. I had to assure him it wasn't cocaine," Arlene said as they all laughed out loud.

"Now we have one more surprise," said Hope.

And with that their curmudgeon waiter of many years carried in an easel and unveiled a caricature of Celeste that would hang on the walls with other legends of Broadway. Then he told them before it was framed, he had tucked in a few ashes so she would forever stay in their favorite dining establish-
~~~~~~

ment.

That was when the tears started, until finally the waiter shouted, “Ladies, snap out of it.”

CHAPTER 37
AND SO IT BEGINS...

It had been a wonderful summer and all too soon Labor Day arrived.

Suzy had spent most of her time with Devon at the beach house. She was able to work remotely and stayed in touch with Amy, and was glad things slow down in July and August. Devon had rebuilt the tasting room at Martinique's and was focused on restoring stability to The Old Barn vineyard after the chaos of the past several months.

Trish and Michael fell in love with the North Fork after several visits and bought a small weekend and summer home not too far from Devon's, so the couples got to spend a lot of time together. And Trish and Michael got to spend time with Tatiana too, who had become like a daughter to them.

By the end of the summer, Ian had asked Tatiana to move in with him, and she accepted. While Trish and Michael knew they would miss her living with them, she had their blessings.

Ian had exciting plans for the fall. Their vines were maturing and would take about three years for their first wine. So, he had decided to open a tasting room, farmers market, and an art gallery to start building their brand. He made a deal with Devon to carry the Martinique and The Old Barn wines in his tasting room. And the art gallery would showcase Tatiana's beautiful watercolors of the North Fork. The grand opening would be later in September.

Jason, Madge, and the children had loved every moment at their farm in Vermont, and especially the month of August when the senate was in recess.

As much as Suzy, Madge, and Trish had enjoyed their summers, there was always something exciting about returning to New York after Labor Day. It was if the whole city springs back to life again. And the first thing on their calendars was Celeste's memorial.

~~~~~~

Hope had rented out the seventeen-hundred-seat Palace Theatre on the first Monday after Labor Day. She had picked Monday when the theaters were dark. Suzy had talked to her several times over the summer as Hope bounced ideas off her. "It's the most important production I've ever done," said Hope, "and I want it to be perfect.

The day was finally here, and the entire theater was packed. The audience included friends, colleagues, and fans who won tickets via a lottery. The Ripe Tomatoes and their significant others had all been seated near the front of the theater. Hope had asked each of them to prerecord a one-minute tribute and she had them edited together.

The memorial opened up with a ten-minute video montage celebrating Celeste's life, while Elton John's "The Circle of Life" from *The Lion King* played in the background. When
~~~~~~

Hope walked onto the stage after the video there wasn't a dry eye in the house.

She had orchestrated a beautiful event, with the right number of speakers and video tributes. They had also recreated one of the last scenes from *If Tomorrow Never Comes* that included the touching monologue penned by Celeste and read by the actor who played the dying character in the play.

"And if tomorrow never comes, I will die happily knowing that I was one of the fortunate ones who found true love, that I was one of the lucky ones who had friends beside me in the good times and the bad times. And I will die happily knowing that I was far from perfect, but I gave it my best. Please do not weep for me when I am gone, but remember me with smiles and laughter when you think about the good times we have shared and toast me with a perfectly dry martini from time to time as well."

After the memorial, the Ripe Tomatoes were part of a small group of Celeste's friends that Sir Oliver had invited back to Celeste's New York City apartment.

Suzy made her way over to Hope and told her what a beautiful event it was. "Celeste would have loved every second of it."

Sir Oliver thanked them all for coming, and especially Hope. "And now we will honor one of Celeste's wishes." As he was talking, the caterers were passing out perfectly dry martinis to each guest.

He lifted his glass, and toasted, "To our beautiful Celeste. May we always remember her with a smile and a laugh when we think of special moments we have each shared with her.

Cheers!"

~~~~~~

It was the last weekend in September, and everyone had returned to the North Fork for the grand opening of the tasting room and the art gallery signally the official launch of Kinnetty Vineyards.

Ian and Suzy had agonized over the name for months. The name and the branding would be very important going forward. One evening in early July, Suzy and Devon were enjoying wine on the porch of the farmhouse with Ian and Tatiana, when she asked what their aunt Millie had been like.

"She was tough as nails," said Suzy, "and didn't suffer fools gladly, but she was also one of the kindest, most giving people I have ever known. She came to this country from Ireland with her parents when she was just a child. In those days the Irish were looked down on, so it wasn't easy in the beginning."

"And where was she from in Ireland?" asked Tatiana.

The second Tatiana asked that question the light bulb went off in Suzy's head.

"That's it! I know what we should call the vineyard."

They all waited.

"Kinnitty Vineyards. Aunt Millie was born in Offaly, in the Midlands Region, which is where our family is from in Ireland. There's a beautiful 19th-century castle there called Kinnitty that's now a hotel. Your dad and I once stayed there."

"Mom, that's perfect," said Ian excitedly.

By the end of the summer, they also had their logo and what would be their very first label. It was a beautiful watercolor of the farmhouse by Tatiana.
~~~~~~

On the eve of the opening, they were all gathered in the tasting room—Trish and Michael, Madge and Jason, Keri and Chris, Suzy and Devon—as Ian uncorked some bottles of sparkling wine from The Old Barn vineyards and Tatiana passed the fluted glasses.

"Thank you to each one of you, who are such an important part of my life, for making today possible. But especially to you, Mom. I won the lottery when I got you for a mom. And to Devon, who took this neophyte wannabe wine guy under your wing."

They all lifted their glasses and did a round of glass clinks.

"And now I have one more thing to make this day even more special." And with that he went down on one knee and took Tatiana's hand in his.

"Tatiana, I love you with all my heart. Will you be my wife?"

Happy tears spilled down her face as she said, "Yes, yes, yes!"

Trish watched Tatiana and Ian. She was so happy for them and realized in that moment that she had never been happier in her life than she was right now. She wanted to hold on to this moment forever. When she and Michael were living a billionaire's life when he was in the hedge fund business, they had things, but nothing had meaning. And when they lost it all and Michael had an affair she was in despair. It was Suzy and Madge who been by her side helping her through those difficult days. But those days had led her and Michael to build a life with real meaning and it was a life she loved.

Madge couldn't get "The Circle of Life" song out of her head and it seemed to be playing so loudly right now she wondered if everyone else could hear it. She had thought about

Celeste's words often since the memorial and all she learned from her, especially her many warnings to Madge to not make her career her life. Oh, how true that turned out to be. Her life with Jason and the children was everything to her. And the fact that she could still tell important stories, but in a more meaningful way now was just the icing on the cake. And Trish and Madge had been her rocks for all these years. How lucky can one girl get?

Suzy looked around the room. It truly was the circle of life. Keri had just told her she was pregnant, and now Ian was getting married. So much had changed in the past couple of years. When Ken had first died, she had days when she didn't want to go on, and it was Trish and Madge who got her through those dark times. And then to have found Devon again and return to the North Fork was a scenario she could never have imagined in a thousand years. Now here were all the people she loved most in the world celebrating this happy day. *I wish Ken could be here to see this.* That's when she looked up at the rafters in the tasting room and saw the red cardinal staring down at her.

ACKNOWLEDGEMENTS

I wrote this book during the COVID-19 pandemic and through those many challenging days that turned into months, I was sustained first and foremost by my husband, Stu Benton, who always keeps me laughing, encourages me in every endeavor, and brings the sunshine to every single day. To my daughter, Roni Jenkins, and my three grandchildren, I am very blessed to have you close by and even when we had to social distance, we could still see each other.

To my amazing friends of more years than I can count—Sandra Russo, Peggy Conlon, Barbara Shimaitis, Maria Watson, Joanne Davis, and Debbie Yount—you are the "original" Tomatoes who always have each other's backs. I thank you for all the laughter, seeing each other through the tears, all the adventures we've had, and for all your support and encouragement over the years. Here's to more adventures to come.

To my partners at The Three Tomatoes who are also dear friends—Debbie Zipp, Anne Akers, Kim Selby, Randie Levine Miller, my daughter Roni Jenkins, and Valerie Smaldone (who believed in us early on and created our first events). They have all helped to build the incredible community of women who proudly call themselves "Tomatoes."

And to all my New York City friends, you inspire me with your beauty, grace, wit, and boundless energy. They include, to name but a few, Judy Katz, Jane Goldman, Gabrielle Carlson, Suzanne Harvey, Grace Richardson, Merrill Stone, Carol Sue Gershman, Judy Davis, Judy Stewart, and Margot Tohn. You are shining examples of living life to the fullest.

ABOUT THE AUTHOR

Cheryl Benton, aka the "head tomato," is founder and publisher of The Three Tomatoes, a digital lifestyle media platform for *women who aren't kids.* Having lived and worked for many years in New York City, the land of size zero twenty-somethings, she was truly starting to feel like an invisible woman. She created The Three Tomatoes as the antidote for invisibility and sent it to 60 friends. Today she has thousands of friends and is chief cheerleader for smart, savvy women who want to live their lives fully at every age and every stage.

She spent her first career in the NYC advertising agency business as a top executive at some of the largest agencies in the world.

She is a graduate of Adelphi University and a recipient of the Distinguished Alumni Award. She was also inducted into the Business Marketing Hall of Fame and was named a top CEO by SmartCEO magazine. She is a frequent speaker on marketing to women, and women's global issues, and is co-author of *Leading Women: 20 Influential Women Share Their Secrets to Leadership, Business, and Life,* Paperback–December 5, 2014, Adams Media.

A wife, mother, and grandmother (her favorite title), she resides in New York with her husband and two dogs. She is author of *Can You See Us Now?* her first novel. She co-wrote two books with her daughter, Roni Jenkins, called *Martini Wisdom* and *More Martini Wisdom.*

To learn more about The Three Tomatoes, visit www.thethreetomatoes.com

If you enjoyed the book, please take a few minutes to write a review at Amazon.